YOU
KNOW
WHAT
YOU
HAVE
TO
DO

# YOU KNOW WHAT YOU HAVE TO DO

BONNIE SHIMKO

AMAZON CHILDREN'S PUBLISHING

*For Lillian*

Amazon Publishing
Attn: Amazon Children's Publishing
P.O. Box 400818
Las Vegas, NV 89140
www.amazon.com/amazonchildrenspublishing

Library of Congress Cataloging-in-Publication Data available upon request.

9781477816424 (hardcover)
1477816429 (hardcover)
9781477866429 (eBook)
B00AOBGZ8G (eBook)

Book design by Abby Kuperstock
Editor: Melanie Kroupa

Printed in The United States of America (R)
First edition
1  2  3  4  5  6  7  8  9  10

Every sweet has its sour, every evil its good.

—RALPH WALDO EMERSON

You know what you have to do.

*I* will always carry the guilt for what I've done. Most days the memories sleep in a dark corner of my mind, but sometimes they wake up and remind me of what a vile person I am. My shrink, Dr. Scott, thinks I'm just anxious and that with therapy I'll be as good as new. I don't even know what good as new feels like because the bad thoughts have been in me forever.

You'd never know from looking at me, though. I'm over there—the tall, skinny, strawberry-blond girl with glasses sitting at the loser table in the Allenburg High School cafeteria. My name is Mary-Magdalene Feigenbaum. No, really. I'm serious. My mother is what you might call a little weird. Plus, she's a professional worrier, so when I was born, she put a lot of thought into what she should call me.

Number one: she wanted people to sit up and take notice when I tell them who I am. She scored A plus on that one. Two: she thinks hyphenated names are highbrow. She must not have thought about Patty-Ann Thurston, the full-grown woman who pedals around town on her gigantic blue tricycle and lifts her shirt for anybody who'll buy her a soda—"A-Peek-for-a-Pepsi Patty" is what the creeps call her. Three: my mother's afraid of death and thinks the religious types have the best chance of getting into heaven since they can unload their sins before they croak. And even though she hasn't seen the inside of a church since I've known her, she chose the name of the most heavy-duty saint she could think of and slapped it on me, which I'm pretty sure is child abuse. Just thinking about it makes my head hurt.

My mother calls me Mary-Magdalene—no exceptions! Most adults call me Mary. My stepfather calls me Mare. The kids at school and my shrink call me Maggie—which is okay for now. But in three years, when I'm eighteen, I'm going to change my name to Alexandra. I think it has a very nice ring to it. A girl could wear a name like that anywhere—even to work as a zoo veterinarian after she graduates from Cornell.

"Let's get outta here," Abigail Flute says as she stuffs her napkin and straw paper into the milk carton on her tray which is still piled high with mystery casserole and anemic-looking string beans. "I have to get my essay from my locker before English."

2

"I have to get mine, too," I reply. I grab what's left of my bag lunch, toss it in the trash can on the way out of the cafeteria, and follow Abigail to the sophomore lockers.

Abigail's been my best friend since eighth grade when her family moved to Allenburg—really my only friend, if you don't count Lester Pint, the class genius who lives at the end of my street, follows me around like a hungry kitten, and slips love notes through the ventilation slots of my locker. Lester's okay, I just wish he didn't like me in a girlfriend way. I've known him forever, and he's more like a brother to me than anything. I don't have the heart to tell him to cool it, though, because I know he'd be crushed.

Abigail's father is the high school principal and her mother teaches math, so Abigail has a double dose of misery to deal with. On top of that, she has to wear a retainer that makes her look like a frog and talk weird. It's funny, though—she doesn't even seem to realize that she's a geek. Or maybe she just doesn't care. Anyway, nobody picks on her because of who her parents are. I don't care that I'm a geek either. In fact, I don't want to be popular, so we're both pretty much invisible, which is fine with me. The fewer people I get close to the better.

ɪ ɪ ɪ

*I love you once. I love you twice. I love you more than cats love mice.* As I shove Lester Pint's latest note in my pants pocket, I think how his poems turned silly and upbeat as soon as his father died. His mother came alive, too, and now spends most of her time working in her flower garden instead of hiding behind closed drapes. Word around town was that Mr. Pint pummeled her even worse than he did his son.

Earlier this year, Lester was standing with me by the school fence until it was time to go in. When I asked him why he looked so angry, he told me how his father, a semifamous artist, had tied his cocker spaniel puppy up in a burlap bag and tossed it into their swimming pool because it had chewed a package of expensive new brushes the UPS guy left on their front step. I thought Lester was making it up, but when I saw the tears in his eyes, I knew he was telling the truth. Then I heard mumbling in my head, and it startled me. I covered my ears and tried to will it away. Until that moment, the only bad thoughts I'd had were how I'd like to yell at Mr. Burdock, our history teacher, for giving us so much homework and then actually tell him how lame his stupid comb-over looks and that it would take more than three strands of hair to camouflage his bald head.

But when Lester told me how his father spent most of his time in his studio behind their house drinking himself into a stupor and then beating his mother to a pulp, a stabbing pain pierced my brain and then a real voice came—a man's voice—one I'd never heard before. Not scary or mean—more low and patient, like a loving father explaining something important to a daughter. And that voice said, *You know what you have to do.*

"No, I don't!" I answered in my mind. "I have no idea what you're talking about!"

*There's no reason to get upset,* the voice replied, gentle. *I'll explain everything step by step—*

⁘

The police investigation ruled it an accident when Mr. Pint's studio went up in flames on Halloween night with him passed out cold on the floor inside. They figured he'd dropped a cigarette and started the fire himself.

But they were wrong. After Lester and I had walked home from a party that night at school, he went inside and I continued down the street toward my house. I was nearly there when the pain in my head returned and so did the voice. *Haven't you forgotten something?* it asked in a singsong tone.

"I don't want to do this," I answered, my voice trembling. "I just want to go home."

*We planned all this yesterday,* the guy in my head said. *That creep is abusing your friend and his mother.* When I didn't say anything, he continued. *And just think of Lester's innocent little puppy. A man that vicious shouldn't be allowed to live.* The guy's voice turned supercalm. *Only you can make things right.*

The pain in my head had gotten so bad, I could hardly stand it, but I circled around to the back of Lester's house. Then I entered Mr. Pint's studio, stepped over his passed-out body, and lit the mess of oily rags he was lying next to with my mother's lighter. The voice had told me to take it from her purse before I left for the party. As soon as the flames started, I hightailed it out of there, and the headache disappeared.

I often wonder if Mr. Pint woke up and tried to escape like Lester's poor little puppy must have. Just the thought of it makes me feel sick to my stomach.

*  *  *

"Get your essay and let's go," Abigail says, tapping me on the shoulder. "We're gonna be late. I said your name a million times. It's like you were in a trance or something. Didn't you hear me?"

I hadn't heard a thing. "Sorry," I say, then point to the paper I'm holding. "I'm just a little nervous about reading this thing to the class."

"I love your stories," Abigail says on our way to English. "I don't know how you come up with all that creepy stuff. You must be related to Stephen King or something."

They've already eaten his head and are ready to go for the rest.

"Roxie?" I yell when I get home from school. Roxie's my mother, but she has this weird idea that if I call her by her first name, people will think we're sisters, which is pretty dumb because we've lived in Allenburg, New York, population next to nothing, since before I was born.

Everybody knows I'm the bastard memento a red-headed jackass named Lonnie Kraft left behind after he got tired of my mother's affection and moved on to a new girlfriend. And everybody knows that Lonnie Kraft now lives ten miles west of here, put away behind the maximum-security bars of the Clinton Correctional Facility for bludgeoning his mother to death with a meat pounder because she cooked his eggs wrong.

"Roxie!" I yell again. Maybe she's downstairs with my step-father, Harry Feigenbaum. Harry's an undertaker, and we live on the second floor of the funeral home.

"I'm down here in the office," Roxie yells back. "Come on. I'll drive you to your appointment."

The appointment she's talking about is with my shrink. She sends me to see Dr. Scott every other Monday because of my nightmares and the screaming that wakes the whole house. I go just to shut her up and because I think maybe it'll quiet the voice in my head that tells me to kill people, even though I keep that part to myself. So far, nothing. The nightmares still come, and Roxie's losing patience with Dr. Scott. I guess she figured I'd be a quick fix. As far as she's concerned, a kid with a normal family couldn't be too screwed up. Yeah, *right*. Maybe *her* family was normal, but she must have forgotten about the nut job who donated half of my DNA.

"Little hustle," Roxie says as I'm heading toward the back step of the funeral home where she's waiting. "I have a hair appointment after I drop you off, and I don't want to be late."

As I come toward her, she gives me her you-are-such-a-dis-appointment face. "How many times have I told you to stand up straight?" she nags. "You look like a pretzel when you're all stooped over like that." Before I can react, she nearly yanks my shoulders out of their sockets as she forces them back. "There, that's better." I slouch even more than before just to see her fume. "Have it your way." She sighs. "You'll never get a boy-friend looking like that."

"Good!" I say, cocky. "I don't want one." This is not exactly true. There's this new boy in school, Jacob Hauser. He doesn't say much to anybody, but I've caught him staring at me a few times in history class. Once he even smiled and I smiled back.

"Of course you want a boyfriend," Roxie says as we head for the garage. "Every girl does."

"Not me. I have a girl friend. That's all *I* want."

I knew that would stop her short. She grabs my arm, and her eyes get as round as moons. "What are you talking about? Are you telling me that you're a lesbian?"

I'm loving this. "Maybe. I'm not sure."

"How can you not be sure about a thing like that?" Her face has actually gone white, and her mouth is stretched out long like a bright red gummy worm.

"And *this* is when you decided to drop the bomb on me— when we don't have time to discuss it?" She's breathing so hard, I think she might have a heart attack.

"Roxie, I'm just messing with you. I was talking about Abigail."

She smacks her hand over her chest and purses her lips tight. "Sometimes I think you want to kill me with your nonsense."

My breath catches in my throat. I don't want to kill my mother; but if it happens, it won't be nonsense that makes me do it.

Now Roxie's got a cigarette in her mouth. She's trying to light it with the pack of matches she took from her purse, but the wind keeps blowing out the flame. "Damn!" she says, dropping another dead match on the driveway. "Are you sure you haven't seen my lighter?"

"I'm sure," I lie. "I've told you that a million times. Why would I need a lighter, anyway? I don't smoke." I add a little venom to the word *I* to remind her that she's the one with the dirty habit. Maybe this will get the attention off me.

"Well, I can't understand how it could have just disappeared like that." She's talking more to herself now than to me. "And it was so expensive: sterling silver with my initials and all. Harry bought it for me at Tiffany's when we all went to New York City for Christmas—the year you turned twelve. That was such a good time. Why, we even went to see . . ."

While she's taking her little trip down Memory Lane, I think about the night I murdered Mr. Pint and why the guy in my head told me to take Roxie's lighter. He said that way I wouldn't leave any evidence, such as a partly burned match that might have a fingerprint on it. But the plan backfired. When the flames jumped toward my face, it freaked me out and I dropped the lighter—complete with Roxie's initials and my fingerprints. I worried for days that the police would find it and arrest me. Then everybody would know what a horrible person I am. But when Mr. Pint's death was ruled an accident, Mrs. Pint had what was left of the shed demolished and hauled away in the back of a dump truck, lighter and all.

"Wasn't that fun?" Roxie's looking at me with excitement in her eyes. I have no idea what she's talking about.

"Wasn't what fun?"

"When we went to Radio City Music Hall. Wasn't that fun?"

"Yes," I say, nostalgic now myself. "Lots of fun." I wish things were as uncomplicated as they were back then.

We start walking again. It's hot for June, and Roxie's all dolled up in yellow capri pants and a matching sleeveless top with sequins sewn along the neckline—both way too tight—and a pair of gold high-heel espadrilles that make her walk as if she's balancing on a tightrope. Roxie loves anything froufrou—the flashier the better. Probably because her life is so dull. She stops and looks as though she's trying to think. "Not that I have anything against lesbians," she says, all gooey sweet. "My best friend in high school was one."

"Who was that?"

"Eleanor West. I told you about her."

"No, you didn't."

"Of course I did. She was the girl who had the affair with the shop teacher, Mr. Traynor, in her senior year and got kicked out of school just before graduation."

"I thought you said she was a lesbian."

"She was for a while, but then she got mixed up with Mr. Traynor."

"Well, then—"

"Oh, never mind. I guess she didn't know what she was. Let's just go."

Roxie's brand-new cherry-red Mustang convertible is parked between the hearse and the long, black mourners' car, which makes her car look even snazzier.

"Careful of the paint!" she snaps as I open the door.

"I'm always careful of the paint," I say, just as snippy. "I'd never want to put a scratch on your *perfect* baby."

She ignores my sarcasm and cranks the key in the ignition. I grab my armrest because I know what's coming next. She shifts, lets out the clutch then puts her foot on the gas. The car leaps backward and stalls. Roxie spews a river of curses. I look over and roll my eyes.

When she doesn't react, I say, "Why didn't you just get an automatic?" Even though I know the answer.

"Stick shifts go with convertibles," she says, as if any moron would know that. "Besides, they're sexier."

*Oh, brother,* I think. *Poor Roxie.* I glance over at her floozied-up self and feel kind of sorry for her. She has all the right equipment to look sexy, pretty even. She just overdoes everything—like she's a coloring-book woman who got scribbled on by a toddler. She hasn't changed her style since her high school graduation photo—the one where the gown hid the fact that she was pregnant with me, which is why she ended up marrying Harry Feigenbaum and why, a lot of times, she treats me like I'm an inconvenience. I guess I'd resent me, too, if I had to marry an older man I didn't love just so I could feed a kid I didn't want.

After a few more tries, Roxie gets the car to cooperate, and we head for Carson Street to Dr. Scott's house, where he has his office.

As I'm getting out of the car, Roxie lowers her sunglasses to peek over at me. "Just tell him what's bothering you, and let's get this over with." Her voice softens a little. "Okay? Whatever it is can't be that bad."

I don't answer.

"Okay?" she repeats. "Just tell him your true thoughts. The nightmares'll go away, and we'll all get a good night's sleep."

I still don't answer, just slam the door and start walking toward the house.

I can hear her sigh ten feet away. "For God's sake, Mary-Magdalene. It's not like you murdered somebody. Just tell him what teenage crap is bugging you and put an end to it!" A few complaints from the transmission, and she peels off down the street.

Her words landed heavy in my gut, and I know there's nothing a therapist or anybody else can do that will fix me. You do not kill a man in cold blood and then talk your way out of it. The only thing you can do is try to live with the guilt.

"How's things, Maggie?" Dr. Scott says when he answers the door. I get a little zing in my heart every time I see him. He's exactly what I would come up with if I had to describe the perfect man: tall, thin, blondish hair, eyes the color of dark polished wood, and a smile that shows teeth so white he could be in a Crest commercial.

After Mr. Pint died, Ms. Diggs, the school counselor, called Roxie to say that I should probably see a professional because I was having more trouble than normal getting over the death of my friend's father. Ms. Diggs figured it was because I lived in a funeral parlor, and the tragedy made home a scary place. Maybe a psychologist could help me realize that sometimes bad things happen and it's nobody's fault. Just because Lester lost a parent doesn't mean I will. Ms. Diggs might be better suited for a different job: a fortune-teller in a circus, maybe. But she's the one who recommended Dr. Scott, so she's okay in my book.

"Any improvement with the nightmares?" Dr. Scott asks as we enter his office. He motions for me to sit on the couch, takes a seat across from me in a green leather armchair, crosses his long legs, and gets his notebook and pen ready.

I sit up straight, pull my T-shirt down tight to draw attention to the fact that my front is fully formed, since that's all I have going for me in the grown-up-woman department. "Yeah, they're almost gone," I lie. I hate talking about my crazies. I'd much rather discuss him. Like how come he isn't married and what does he do in this great big old house when he's not listening to people bellyache about their problems and does he have a girlfriend? When I see him around town, he's always alone.

His look turns serious. "Your mom called and said they're getting worse."

Rats! Why can't Roxie stay out of this? The last thing I want is for Dr. Scott to think I'm nuts. "I guess I've had a couple," I say, sheepish.

"She said it's at least twice a week." He keeps his voice calm and acts as if having screaming fits in the middle of the night is as common as mud.

"Maybe." I shrug. "I just don't remember." I remember all

right, every single, horrible detail about that night in Mr. Pint's studio.

He taps the notebook with his pen. "Since we've been working together for almost six months and we haven't made much headway just talking, I was thinking we might try something new."

"Like what?" I hope he doesn't want to hypnotize me so I'll spill my guts.

"You've probably heard of the Rorschach test."

"No, but I hate tests. I'm terrible at them." That's not true, because the only subject I'm dense in is math. The rest of the stuff is pretty easy. "I don't really want to take a test." I let out a laugh that sounds as fake as it is. "I get enough of those in school." I wonder how old he is . . . twenty-eight, maybe. That's not too much older than me—a May-September relationship.

"It's also called the inkblot test. It's just a bunch of pictures. I'll show them to you, and you'll tell me what you see." He smiles. "I don't put a lot of stock in it; but you're a hard nut to crack, so it's worth a try."

"Oh, okay," I say. "That doesn't sound so bad." I know what the inkblot test is. Everybody does. They use it to see how messed-up weird you really are.

"Well, then. Why don't we give it a try?" He reaches for a stack of big white cards on the table next to him.

I scooch around a little on the couch and take in a big breath like I'm getting ready to do my best. If we were married, we could sit together on this couch and watch movies on TV. I wonder if he likes popcorn—the microwave kind with butter. Of course, I'd let him decide how much salt to put on.

He hands me a card and says, "What does that look like?"

*It looks like two buzzards holding down a man in a black coat. They've already eaten his head and are ready to go for the rest.* I keep my face plain and say in a regular voice, "I see a couple of birds at a feeder, and they're singing to each other. I think they're in love."

Dr. Scott writes my answer on his pad, then hands me the next card. "How about this one?"

*It's a boy holding a dead puppy. The boy is crying.* "I see two little kids playing patty-cake."

More writing. Another card. "And this?"

*Twin girls lighting a sleeping man on fire.* "Two ladies stirring pudding in a pot. And there's a butterfly in the middle—a pretty one."

"How about here?"

*Mr. Pint's charred body coming toward me with his arms out in front of him ready to strangle me.* I try to slow my breathing and smile a little but I can feel my mouth twitching, and a trickle of sweat is making its way down the middle of my back. "I don't see anything. It just looks like spilled ink."

Lots of writing this time—probably that I'm a big, fat fake. "Okay, I think that's enough," Dr. Scott says, a little impatient. He takes the card from my hand, puts it with the ones he didn't use, and leans back in his chair. "How about we discuss you and your mom?"

It feels good to have the attention off me. My shoulders relax. "What about her?"

"Well, every time I've brought her up, you've never had much to say."

I shrug. "There isn't really much *to* say. She's just . . . I don't know . . . a mother."

"How 'bout we try it?" he persists.

"What do you want to know?"

"Anything you want to tell me."

Boy, could I give him an earful. Instead, I give her a break. "She cleans a lot."

"How so?"

"I don't know. She just thinks everything's dirty, so she cleans." I don't add that she warns me a million times a day not to sit on public toilets or drink from water fountains. And I certainly don't tell him about how lately the voice in my head has been saying that she was a slut when she was in high school. That she had sex with any boy who smiled at her. The guy in my head talks with a north-country twang, so I know he's from around here.

"She's worried about germs, then," Dr. Scott says, while scribbling on his pad.

This is the first time I've thought about it, but maybe all that cleaning is her way of trying to wash away her past. Then I wonder what Lonnie Kraft's voice sounds like. He grew up in the next town. Does he have a north-country twang? Is he the one who's putting bad thoughts in my head? I've seen movies where stuff like that happens. I have his blood running through my veins. Maybe that's all it takes.

"Maggie?" Dr. Scott's leaning forward in his chair, looking at me with concerned eyes. He reaches over to touch my hand, and when he does, the cuff of his shirt slides back. He has the perfect amount of hair on his arm: medium.

"Yes?"

"I spoke to you several times, and you didn't answer. What were you thinking about?"

"Just all the homework I have. Sorry, I didn't hear you."

"You know, Maggie," Dr. Scott says in a sympathetic tone, "it seems very hard for you to let your real feelings out one-on-one. I was thinking that you might benefit from group therapy. Maybe if you saw how other people opened up, it would be easier for you."

Not in a million years! "I don't want to discuss my personal life with a bunch of other kids."

"You wouldn't have to say a thing, just listen. And actually, the group I'm thinking of putting you in is mostly adults, but they all have things they're afraid of."

He didn't add "just like you," but I know that's what he meant.

"Join in about their problems if you feel like it. It might prime the pump and then we can go back to individual sessions."

"So I won't have to say anything?"

"Not a word."

"Do I have to give my name?"

"You can make one up."

"But they'll know who I am. This town is so small."

"I doubt it. This group is bused down from Folsom Falls. They don't have a therapist there, so I'm it."

Folsom Falls is about an hour north of Allenburg, and I don't know anybody there. Besides, that'd sure beat sitting here week after week trying to act not crazy so Dr. Scott will like me. Plus, I'd still be able to see him, and Roxie would think I'm trying to get a grip on my teenage crap. "I guess it'd be okay."

*ı ı ı*

As usual, Roxie's late picking me up. I'm on Dr. Scott's front step when she arrives and honks the horn, even though she can see me. "Come on, Mary-Magdalene. We have to get you to swim practice."

I love to swim. That's where I get a chance to shine. Nobody can catch me in the breaststroke, and I'm second best in the butterfly. When I'm in the water, my real life floats away, and my stubborn brain leaves me alone.

"How was your session?" Roxie asks as soon as I'm in the car.

"Good. It was good. Dr. Scott's putting me with a group from now on, so I guess he thinks I'm almost cured."

"That's great!" Roxie says with a genuine smile. "I knew it wasn't very serious."

"Nah," I say. "Not serious at all."

*Do it now! Before he gets away!*

*I*t's Saturday morning, and I'm lying in bed with my basset hound, Maud, trying to decide what I'm going to do today. Abigail's gone to Maine with her parents for the weekend, so I'm on my own. At least Roxie won't be on my back about cleaning my room or doing homework. When the weather's nice, she spends Saturdays antiquing, mostly in Vermont, and doesn't get home until late. And I have to give her this much, she has really upscale taste when it comes to decorating. Feigenbaum's Funeral Home is *the* place to be laid out if you want to impress people.

Maud's sleeping on her back with her feet in the air, which

is what she does when she's supercomfortable. She's snoring big-time with little yips thrown in now and then, and her feet are running in place. She's probably dreaming about Stanley, the hot-looking Doberman down the street she flirts with through the fence when I take her for a walk.

I'm reaching for the novel on my nightstand when I hear *clink* against my window. I know without even looking that it's Lester Pint, and I ignore him like I always do. The funeral home creeps him out. He won't even call here, so instead of ringing the doorbell like a normal person, he tosses stones at my window. I guess he thinks he's Cyrano de Bergerac.

Just as I'm starting chapter three of *Ethan Frome*, Roxie barges in—doesn't knock or anything. Today she's wearing shorts and a halter top, matching leather sandals with bright red hearts on the toes. "I'm leaving now," she says all upbeat. "I left a list of chores for you on the kitchen table. And there's a fruit smoothie in the fridge." Roxie's on a health-food kick, which will last about a week until she reads somewhere that fat and carbs are the way to go; and she'll follow that path until her pants won't zip. Then it'll be the pickle diet or flavored water or some other crazy fad till the weight falls off again.

Another stone against the window.

"What's that racket?" Roxie asks. She goes over and peeks out. "Oh. It's that poor Pint boy. I wonder what he wants."

"Me," I say with no enthusiasm at all.

"What?"

"He has a crush on me."

Roxie stands there staring, as if somebody liking me would be impossible. "Well, what's wrong with that?" she says. "I think it's kind of romantic the way he's trying to get your attention. Like that Steve Martin movie I loved so much—the one with my name in it." She starts to open the blinds.

"Stop!" I plead. "I don't want him to know I'm home."

"Why not? He seems like a nice boy, and he probably needs somebody to talk to after all he's been through." Then her voice changes to no-nonsense. "You were so rattled by what happened to his father, you ended up seeing a psychologist; just imagine what that kid must feel having his own father burned to a crisp like that."

He feels a lot better about it than I do. "I don't want to lead him on is all."

"He probably just wants you to be his friend."

"No," I complain. "He wants me to be his girlfriend." Roxie's nagging woke up Maud, so I give her a belly rub. She licks my arm like it's the sweetest thing she's ever tasted.

"How do you know he likes you in a romantic way?"

I think of his last note, which had gone from silly to disturbing: how he said he had loved me since the seventh grade and that he knew in his heart we'd spend the rest of our lives together. "I just do."

Roxie pulls up the blinds, opens the window, leans out, and gives Lester a big wave. "Hi there!" she calls down. "Are you looking for Mary-Magdalene?"

"Yes! Is she there?"

"She's here. She's just not dressed. Would you like me to tell her something?"

He probably wants me to spend the day in the public library while he works on the science project he's doing for the class he's taking at the community college. He's so crazy smart that he'll graduate high school a year early, and the Ivy League colleges are already recruiting him. I've made up an excuse every time he's asked me to go, but he doesn't give up.

"I was wondering if she wanted to go for a hike."

Well, that's what I call out of the blue. I most certainly do not want to go for a hike or anyplace else with him.

"A hike?" Roxie says.

"I need to get rock samples and hopefully a fossil or two for a project I'm doing for my college class. My mother'll drive us to Sullivan's Mountain and pick us up this afternoon. She'll even pack us a lunch."

"Just a minute," Roxie says, holding up her hand like a traffic cop, which showcases the fake nails all polished perfectly: bright red to match her outfit. "I'll ask her."

She looks at me with big old cow eyes.

I screw my face tight and talk through clenched teeth. "Don't even think about it."

"Why don't you go, Mary-Magdelene?" she whines. "A boy that smart is sure to be successful. He'll probably grow up to be a doctor or lawyer or something big like that."

"He's going to be a cell biologist and try to discover a cure for Alzheimer's disease because his grandmother has it."

"Well, see? Look how thoughtful he is. And I bet those cell biology fellows make a ton of money." She glances back down at Lester. "I'm not crazy about his long hair, but he can cut that." She gives me a pleading look. "Do it for me?"

"Do what for you?"

"Take a hike! Give him a chance."

"I just don't like him in that way."

"So? You'll get to like him." The same as she did Harry Feigenbaum. "And he lives in that beautiful big house with the huge pool. If you're lucky, he'll ask you to swim in it someday. You can show him how good you are."

He already knows how good I am. He comes to every single one of my meets and stares at my boobs. "He's afraid of the water and doesn't know how to swim."

"Well, then you can teach him."

Maud's standing next to Roxie now with her front feet on the windowsill and her tail's slapping against Roxie's bare calf. "She'll have to take her dog," she says to Lester. "I'm going to be gone all day, and my husband's at a casket convention till this afternoon."

"That's okay," I hear Lester say. "We'll meet her in front of your house in an hour."

I walk over to the window in time to see Lester running in the direction of his house, all pigeon-toed and loose as if his bones aren't connected. Then I give Roxie the dirtiest look I can come up with.

"Hiking sounds like fun," she says as if she knows what she's talking about.

"Well then, why don't *you* go?" I snap. "Then *you* can swim in Lester's pool. Besides, I have to babysit tonight."

Roxie gives me her that's-enough look, and I know I've lost the battle. "It'll do you good to get outside," she adds. "And you should be happy that a nice boy asked you to go somewhere. Plus, you don't have to babysit until six o'clock."

She probably thinks her snide little hints about how unpopular I am slip right by me. I'd love to rub her loose-girl past in her face, but I don't. She could have given me away when Lonnie Kraft took off. Instead, she married Harry and sacrificed her happiness so I could have a fantastic father and everything I'll ever need.

*ı ı ı*

"We have to sign in over there and write down how long we're staying." Lester's pointing at a clipboard nailed to a pine tree. Above the clipboard is a No Hunting notice with what looks like a bullet hole smack in the middle of the word *No*.

"Have you been here before?" I ask, trying to keep Maud from pulling my arm off. Even at home she spends most of our walks with her nose to the sidewalk, tracking other dogs and whatever else might have walked there. But here she's in hound heaven and ready to go.

"No," he says, "but I researched mountain protocol and etiquette on the web."

Why doesn't that surprise me?

"Then when we leave, we sign out," he adds. "If we're still here at the end of the day, somebody'll come looking for us before it gets dark."

The last thing I want to do is sleep under a tree with Lester Pint, so I say, "Let's go sign in!"

"We're the only ones here," Lester says as he's writing our names and phone numbers on a faded, dog-eared paper. "This mountain's not that popular. It's only about half a mile to the top. I guess most people want more of a challenge."

Good! We'll be finished when Mrs. Pint picks us up at two, and there'll still be most of the afternoon left to read or work on the story I'm writing—the one about the perfect girl who is so good-hearted that she is going to spend her life taking care of poor little orphans.

*

Another hard yank from Maud. "Are we going or not?" I ask Lester as he stands there adjusting the safety strap on his glasses so they won't fly off while he's doing something as dangerous as walking along a trail.

Lester's expression looks more tentative than usual, and he's clearing his throat like he does when he's nervous. Then the muscles in his face ease up as though he's just solved his problem. "Why don't you go first?" he says, bowing and pointing the way with his arm outstretched. I guess now he thinks he's Sir Galahad.

He's not fooling me. "Afraid of snakes, huh?" I say, sarcastic.

"I am not!" He overdoes his protest, so I know he's lying. "I just think it should be ladies first."

Oh, brother. I could be home washing the hearse or vacuuming the casket room or one of the million other things on Roxie's list of things for me to do this weekend. It'd be way better than this.

*  *  *

When we reach the top, we're the only ones here. Lester's sitting on a rock under a tree, going through the plastic sandwich bags that are filled with the treasures he found on the way up, neatly labeled and stored in his backpack. I hand him Maud's leash and start for the edge of the cliff to see how far down it goes.

"Don't get too close," Lester warns as if he's my mother. Well, not *my* mother, but a regular one who'd worry about her kid falling off a mountain.

"I'll only be a minute," I say, inching my way to the brink. "Wow! I didn't realize it was such a steep drop-off. The only thing you can see down there are rocks and trees. Why don't you come on over and look?"

Lester scoots back on his rock and grabs hold as if he thinks I might pull him off and drag him to the edge. "That's okay. I've seen enough trees for one day."

I don't get on him for being afraid of cliffs because he's been almost fun to be with: no show-off lessons about science junk like I thought there would be. "Then let's head to the bottom and eat lunch while we wait for your mother to come get us."

We're just a little way down the mountain when a guy comes out of the woods with a rifle slung over his shoulder. He's about Harry's age and filthy, like he hasn't had a shower or brushed his teeth—ever. He's carrying a plastic Walmart bag. It's heavy with something and smeared with blood. "What are you doing on *my* mountain?" he snarls. "Nobody's allowed here. Why don't you go climb one of the high peaks like everybody else?"

Lester sidesteps toward me. "I needed some stuff for a science project, and this is close to where we live," he says real fast. His chin is actually quivering. I bet he's remembering how his father used to bawl him out. "I didn't know this mountain belonged to anybody."

"He's just messing with you," I say, snotty. "Nobody owns a mountain."

Fast as a snap, the man drops the Walmart bag and points the barrel of the rifle at my face. "Got a smart-ass mouth, huh?" he says, all big shot. "Just so happens I'm the last of the Sullivans. Used to be there was family all over this place till the state stole it—paid us peanuts for all this land." Nests of tea-colored spit have settled in the corners of his mouth, which, for some cockeyed reason, makes me more nervous than the gun. "Then everybody moved away 'cept me." Now he's tapping the bag with the toe of his boot. "I'm on my way home to make me a nice rabbit stew."

You'd think I'd be petrified, but I don't feel anything except a tiny pain in the back of my head—the same pain I felt when I learned about the things Lester's father did.

"Goddamned stupid mutt!" the man yells at Maud, who's sniffing the bloody bag. "Keep away!" Then he points the rifle at *her* head and pulls back a lever on the top of the barrel.

I drop to my knees and cover Maud with my body. *Now* I'm scared. Maud's never hurt anybody in her whole life, and I'd much rather get killed than have to live without her.

"Ah, just get out of here," the man says, disgusted. From the corner of my eye, I see him back away then pick up the Walmart bag. "And don't come back!"

"We won't," Lester whines as I'm getting to my feet. "We promise."

As I watch Mr. Sullivan walk up the trail, my pain gets worse. The voice in my head is slow and deliberate. *You know what you have to do.*

"Let's go!" Lester says in a loud whisper. He grabs my shirt-sleeve and starts down the mountain.

"Wait a minute," I answer. I make a big production of checking my pants pockets. "Damn! I must have dropped my cell phone when we were at the top."

"Well, forget about it. That crazy guy's probably up there already."

"I can't forget about it. My mother'll kill me. It's brand-new."

"Why'd you bring it, anyway? There's no service in the mountains."

"Well, I didn't know that. Besides, that jerk said he was

29

going home. I'll just be a minute. You take Maud, and I'll catch up with you."

"But he's got a gun."

"Yeah, and if he really wanted to kill us, he would have."

"I think he *would* have killed Maud," Lester says, patting the dog's back. "If you hadn't protected her."

I nod. Then the man in my head gets impatient. *Do it now! Before he gets away!*

I give Maud a scratch behind her ear and look at Lester. "You go. I'll meet you at the bottom."

*ı ı ı*

When I reach the top of the mountain, the guy is there, standing by the edge of the cliff and aiming his rifle toward a bunch of birds in the sky. He startles when he hears me, backs away from the ledge a little. "What do you want?" he growls. "I thought I told you to scram."

"I'm going, but I think I left my phone up here."

"I didn't see a phone."

"Is it okay if I just look around?"

"Yeah, but hurry it up."

I pretend I'm searching the ground, and he inches to the edge again so the tree isn't in the way and he can see the sky. Then I look up and ask, "What kind of birds are those?"

"They're mallard ducks," he instructs with superiority in his voice.

"Ah," I say with a tone that sounds as though I'm impressed

by his knowledge of nature. "But even if you *hit* one, it'd land way down on those rocks. How would you get it?"

He looks at me as if I'm the biggest fool he's ever met. "I'm not killing them for food. I'm using them for target practice."

Hearing him say that makes my headache even worse.

"This is nothing," he goes on, bragging. "You ought to be here in April when the Canada geese come through on their way north. They fly in a V formation and honk their heads off. They're so loud you can't hear yourself think. Stupid birds. They should stay in Florida and save themselves all this trouble." He laughs, mean. "But then I'd miss out on a whole bunch of fun."

"What kind of fun?"

"I aim for the leader. It's a blast to see the rest of them go bonkers till they choose a new one. It's like watching a fifty-car pileup."

The pain in my head is now booming, and I think my skull's about to explode.

While the guy's taking aim at a duck, he says, "You know I wouldn't have really shot you back there. I was just trying to scare you. I'd never kill a person."

I stand next to him and fake a laugh. "I know that. But what about my dog? Would you have killed her?" My voice is all sweet and innocent, not accusing, just wondering.

His cheek is smashed tight against his rifle, and he's staring into the lens at another flock of birds heading toward us. "Animals are different," he says, cocky. "They don't count. Even God said, 'Let man have dominion over the fish of the sea, and over the fowl of the air, and over the cattle, and over all the earth, and over every creeping thing that creepeth upon the earth.'" He looks over at me, serious. "That means we can do whatever we want to them, and it's not a sin."

"Right," I say as if I agree with him. "Oh, good! There's my phone under that leaf." I walk behind him, crouch, and pretend I'm picking up something. The inside of my mouth has gone as dry as dust, and my heart's pounding so hard I expect it to burst wide-open.

The guy's body stiffens when the birds are right above us. He holds the gun tighter. "Watch that big fellow in the front take a dive!" he brags.

Just before he pulls the trigger, I stand up and shove him— hard! I don't see him land because of all the pines, but I know he'll never hurt another animal.

Then my body calms down, and my head clears as I watch the ducks fly off. Safe.

*　*　*

When I get to the bottom of the mountain, I rip the sign-in paper off the clipboard, ball it up, and shove it into my pocket. Then I look for Lester.

"Did you find your phone?" he asks as I plop down next to him under a gigantic pine.

"Nah. I must have lost it on the way up. Or maybe I *did* leave it at home and just forgot."

"Was that guy up there?"

I shake my head. "Uh-uh. No sign of him."

Lester points to his backpack. "How about some lunch?"

"No thanks," I say. "I'm not hungry."

When you have just killed a man, eating is the last thing on your mind.

Shut her up for good!

*I*'m two doors down from my house, babysitting for Ali Rogers, who I've taken care of since she was born eight months ago. I love babysitting for her because she's so cute and sweet and I can pretend that she's my baby. Besides being a veterinarian, I want to get married someday and have a whole bunch of kids. And believe me, they are going to have normal first names, no hyphens.

Ali's asleep upstairs, and I'm sitting on the couch watching TV and talking to Abigail on my cell phone.

"Just a sec," Abigail says; "my mother's calling me. I'll be right back."

While I'm waiting, my mind goes back to that cliff on Sullivan's Mountain. I think how Ali's mother would feel if she knew that she'd left her baby with a girl who'd killed a man just a few hours ago. Then I look at my fingernails that I've bitten down to nubs. I can't believe I left the Walmart bag at the edge of the cliff. If the body is found, that's where the police will look first. Nobody would believe Mr. Sullivan fell off a mountain he's lived on his entire life. Plus, Maud's DNA is all over that bag from when she was sniffing it.

"Okay, I'm back," Abigail says. "My mother made brownies."

I can hear her chewing and think how hungry I am. "You're so lucky," I say. "The only thing they have here is healthy stuff like yogurt and figs."

Abigail makes a *yuck* sound. "So what are you doing tomorrow?" she asks. "Want to come over to my house?"

"Sure." I'm about to tell her about Jacob and how cute I think he is when I hear Ali crying. "I have to go upstairs and get the baby," I say. "I'll see you tomorrow. I have something I want to tell you."

"What's the matter, Ali?" I say as I enter her room. "Are you hungry?" Her hands are balled into little pink fists, and she's crying so hard even cradling her doesn't help. "It's okay, sweetie. We'll get you some milk." After I've changed her, I pick her up and head for the stairs. As I'm walking down the hall, my head starts throbbing. Then the man's voice spooks me. *Nobody should have to listen to that howling!*

What?! Not now! Oh, please, God. Not sweet little Ali.

The man's voice screeches in my head. *Throw the brat down the stairs!*

This is the first time he's ever told me to hurt an innocent person. I stop and look at Ali's little face: all scrunched-up red. Her mouth is wide-open, and the two tiny teeth on the bottom, the only ones she has, remind me of miniature Chiclets. Everything about her is so new and perfect, and she smells like heaven must smell.

The guy's voice roars. *Shut her up for good! You know what you have to do.*

I start walking toward the stairs again as though in a trance, and I'm nearly there when Ali stops crying, reaches up, and pats my cheek with her chubby little hand. Then she smiles and makes babbling sounds.

*Throw her!* the voice hollers. *What are you waiting for?* The guy has never spoken to me in an ugly tone before today, and it scares me. I stop walking, and before the voice has a chance to say anything more, I hurry back to Ali's room and lay her in her crib. She stares up at me as if I've lost it; and when I just stand there, she starts to scream, even louder than before.

I run downstairs and call Harry. "I can't make Ali stop crying." I'm gasping because I can't take a full breath. "Will you come over—*now*?!"

Harry's voice is garbled with sleep. "Be right there."

*   *   *

When Harry arrives, I'm waiting for him on the porch, as far away from Ali as I dare go.

"Where's the baby?" he asks.

"She's upstairs in her crib."

Harry looks confused, but he doesn't get on me for leaving Ali alone in the house. Instead, he says, "Well, let's go see if we can find out what the little lady wants."

"She's hungry," I tell Harry as I motion for him to go inside ahead of me.

I'm trembling, and I guess it shows in my voice because Harry takes my hand; and in the glow of the porch light, he stares at me so intently, it's as though he can see clear through to my soul. "What happened in there?" he asks. "Why are you so upset?"

This is the closest anybody's ever gotten to my secret, and I have to steer him away from it, not let him know that my heart is as black as the devil's. "It's the crying. I can't stand that tinny, high-pitched noise." Then I make my voice sound matter-of-fact. "I've decided that I don't want to babysit anymore."

"But you've always loved taking care of kids."

"I used to," I say, trying to swallow the lump in my throat. I know I can't go anywhere near them from now on. And the fact that I'm not safe around children makes me so sad that I have to hold back tears.

"You said you couldn't wait to have kids of your own."

"I've changed my mind." There's no way I could ever be anybody's mother.

As we enter the house, there's pure silence; and for a quick second, I imagine that the voice had turned into a real person and strangled Ali or smothered her with her blanket. But when I come back to reality, I say, "Harry, will you go upstairs and get the baby? It's the last door on the left."

"Sure, but it sounds as though she went back to sleep."

"Will you bring her down?" I have to know that she's still alive, but I can't go up there.

Harry heads toward the stairs. "I will, but I can't see the point in waking a sleeping baby."

"Just *do* it, *okay*?" I surprise myself because I've never sassed Harry before.

"All right." The words come out a tiny bit annoyed; but the look he gives me is worried, as if he thinks I'm on the road to Crazytown. What he doesn't know is that I've already arrived.

Then Ali's crying starts up again, and relief flows through me like a transfusion.

"Guess I was wrong," Harry calls down. "You'd better get a bottle ready."

*   *   *

On Sunday morning, the smell of bacon cooking wakes up Maud, and she paws at my arm. I ignore her at first, but then she moves on to phase two: sliming my face with her huge, warm tongue. I turn over and bury my head in the pillow. She burrows in and starts washing my ear, which is really yucky, so I give up. Anybody who thinks dogs aren't smart is nuts!

"Morning, Mare," Harry says as I enter the kitchen. "You don't look very chipper." Harry's already dressed: shirt and tie, black pants and shoes. His assistant is off on Sunday, so Harry has to be ready in case somebody decides to croak and he has to make a pickup and console the family.

"I don't feel very chipper," I say, sliding onto a counter stool. I'm picturing that Sullivan guy dead on the rocks and wonder if anybody will even miss him. There was nothing about him on last night's news.

Harry hands me a glass of fresh-squeezed orange juice. "Well, babysitting can tire a girl out."

I've seen pictures of Harry when he was young, and he was a little bit good-looking. Now he's round and faded, and most of his gray hair is gone. But he has the kindest eyes I've ever seen. I love that he refuses to wear the brown rug Roxie bought to camouflage his bald head and make him look younger. Best of all, he treats me as if I'm the daughter he's always wished for.

"Thanks again for last night, Harry," I say after I've gulped down the OJ.

"Glad to help," he says in a cheery voice—no sign of how weird I was acting at Ali's house. Now he's beating a bowl of eggs, getting ready to pour them into a pan. He's an amazing cook, and he's taught me everything he knows, so if the funeral business ever goes under, we could open a fancy restaurant—no sweat.

"I just wish it hadn't been so late," I add. Harry goes to bed right after the eleven-o'clock news.

"Not a problem. I was still awake." I know he's lying to make me feel better. As soon as the omelet's cooking, he says, "I'm going to go wake up your mother. I'll be right back."

*♩ ♩ ♩*

"What smells so good?" Roxie asks as she walks into the kitchen. She's wearing a light-blue terry cloth robe, and her face has taken on a soft look because it's washed and natural. She can relax around Harry because she knows he's not judging her. I hope someday she realizes that she doesn't have to hide behind all that makeup. She heads toward the stove, peeks in the pan. "Oh, good. An omelet." She looks at Harry. "Is it cheese and mushroom?"

"What else?" he answers, playful.

Harry and Roxie have separate bedrooms, and there's never any outward romantic affection. But it works for them. She treats him with respect, and he seems happy to be a father to her, too.

Roxie sits on the stool next to mine and says, "So what's this I hear about no more babysitting for you?"

I reach over, grab a piece of toast off the pile Harry just buttered, and take a big bite to give myself a minute. "I'd just rather do other things," I say after I swallow.

Harry hands Roxie a glass of orange juice, and she takes a sip. "What other things?" she says in a bland tone, as if I might have decided to take up stamp collecting.

I haven't the slightest idea, and I can't think of anything else, so I blurt out, "Well, the end-of-school dance is this coming

Saturday." Rats! Why'd I say that? Now Roxie'll get all nuts and make me go. I'd rather eat dirt than go to a dance.

Harry looks over with anticipation on his face. I think he's been worried about me being a wallflower for the rest of my life almost as much as Roxie has. "Is it for the whole school?" he asks.

"No, just the sophomores." I smile at Harry and say, "It's a fifties theme, so we have to wear antique clothes from the Dark Ages."

Harry laughs. "Watch it, smarty-pants. You know very well that was *my* heyday. I've got pictures around here somewhere of me with my ducktail hairdo and white buck shoes."

I can't imagine Harry as a greaser doing the jitterbug, but I'm glad he had fun. He laughs again and play-jabs me in the arm.

"You can't beat those rock 'n' roll tunes," he continues, but then hesitates for a minute. "You've heard me play my records since you were a baby."

"I know," I tease. I hold my hand two feet from the floor and repeat what I've heard Harry say a zillion times: "'She's just a little tot, but she knows the titles of all the songs and does a great Elvis impersonation.'"

Harry shakes his head. "You were the cutest thing I've ever seen, shaking your little tushy and playing the air guitar." He looks at Roxie. "Wasn't she?"

Roxie rolls her eyes but smiles and nods in agreement about how adorable I used to be. Then she shifts around on her seat and looks straight at me. "Do you have a date?"

"No."

"Maybe that nice Pint boy will ask you."

"He already did." I think of Lester's stupid locker note: *Hey, daddy-o. They're having a sock hop. How 'bout we go?* Then he finished it off with his usual x's and o's, plus a bunch of hearts with wings attached.

"What did you say to him?" Roxie asks.

"I said no." If Jacob Hauser had asked me, I would have said YES! in a hot second.

"Why? Because you got so many better offers?" Roxie's tone is pure furious.

"*No*, because Miss Hanson asked me to be in charge of refreshments, and I said okay." That's a lie, but I know she'd be happy if I would. Nobody else is pathetic enough to take that job. Well, nobody except Abigail, but even she wouldn't do it.

I guess just the fact that I'm going is enough for Roxie. She starts shoveling omelet into her mouth and gets all excited around the eyes. "After breakfast we'll go to the vintage store and get you an outfit. We'll see if we can find one of those poodle skirts and a pair of saddle shoes. You know, like the girls wore in the *American Graffiti* movie."

"I didn't see that one." I don't *want* to see that one.

"Well, you should rent it." Roxie looks at me all serious. "Then you'll know how to act at the dance."

I roll my eyes so huge, it feels as if they're about to pop

right out of my head; but Roxie doesn't notice. She's too busy figuring out ways to make me popular.

Sometimes you wake up and it's a glorious Sunday. Then, before you know it, you've talked yourself into a mess and the whole day is ruined.

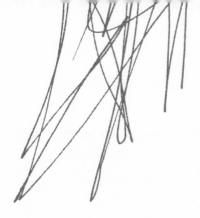

You might as well be a cafeteria lady.

I t's Sunday afternoon, and I'm standing on Abigail's front porch, waiting for her to answer the bell.

Mrs. Flute opens the door. "Hello, Mary," she says, not exactly friendly but not mean either. She's a pretty woman with short, blond hair and dark-brown eyes—no makeup. Her breath smells like Listerine. And Abigail is pure weird. She tells her mother every little thing as if they are best girl friends. "Are you here to see Abigail?" Mrs. Flute asks.

Well, duh. Why else would I have come? "Yes. Is she here?" I know she's here. She never goes anywhere without her parents or me.

"Come in, and I'll go upstairs and check." Before I take a

step, she looks down at my feet and clears her throat, which means "Don't forget your shoes." I slip off my flip-flops and leave them on the welcome mat. I've known since the first time I came here to take off my shoes, and I would have done it now; but I guess reminding me makes Mrs. Flute feel like a big deal. Being friends with Abigail is hardly worth the effort because of her mother. Roxie may be strange, but she would never make a guest feel like a jerk over a nothing thing like that.

"I'll be back in a minute," Mrs. Flute says, and heads for the staircase that has one of those banisters where the spindles are white but the top part is dark wood that ends in a flat curl at the bottom. This house is huge, and you can tell that it must have been gorgeous in its earlier years. But boy, Mrs. Flute could really use Roxie's decorating talent. You do not put plaid curtains in a Victorian home.

I watch Mrs. Flute walk up the stairs, and I am so glad that I will never have her for a teacher because she is famous for being strict. She only gets the advanced placement kids like Lester and Abigail, so being dismal in math has its advantages.

As I'm waiting for Mrs. Flute to come back, I wonder how Abigail will react when I tell her about Jacob.

"Abigail said to go on up," her mother tells me on her way down the stairs. "She's doing some research on the Internet, but she's almost finished."

ı ı ı

Abigail is not doing research. She is standing in front of her full-length mirror, brushing her hair. It is long and wavy and streaky blond, and this is the first time I have seen it not in a ponytail. Someday when her teeth are finished, that girl is going to be a knockout. She has a pastel face—pale skin like the porcelain dolls she keeps in a glass case by her closet, light-blue eyes, and rose-colored cheeks and lips, natural.

"Your mother said you were doing homework," I say when Abigail sees me come in.

"I know. Whenever I hear her footsteps heading toward my room, I get on the computer to look like I'm studying." She rolls her eyes like her mother is finally getting on her nerves. "The only thing she cares about is school."

Well, this whole visit is plain nuts. Maybe I'm in the wrong house. Abigail usually *is* on the computer doing homework, even when she could be doing something fun. And I've never once seen her roll her eyes about her mother. "She's been driving me crazy lately," Abigail adds. "She thinks I should be studying for the SATs every single second." Even with all those *s* words, her enunciation is perfectly clear because her retainer is on the table next to her bed. I've never seen her take it out except when she's eating.

Abigail twists her hair into a ponytail and sits on her bed.

I plop down next to her and say, "You are not going to believe the mess I'm in."

"What mess?"

I tell her about having to go to the dance.

She stares at me with wide eyes. "Just tell your mother you changed your mind."

"I can't. You know how she is."

"Well, you *can't* be the refreshment girl. You might as well be a cafeteria lady."

This is the first time I've heard Abigail talk mean about anybody. I think of our cafeteria ladies with their hairnets and big spoons and canned peas and how they put up with jerks who make snotty comments. Yet those women still manage to smile while they're asking if we'd like tartar sauce with our fish sticks.

Abigail's undone her ponytail and is brushing her hair again. She holds out the strand she's working on and inspects it as if she's seeing how gorgeous it is for the first time. It's as though I'm watching a butterfly emerge from its dull gray cocoon, and it's making my insides feel weird—as if she's outgrowing me.

"Aren't you going to put your retainer in?" I ask, hoping she'll say yes. "You're supposed to wear it all the time, right?"

"Not anymore. The dentist said my teeth are perfect. Now I just have to wear it at night." She gives me a big smile, and she's right. Her teeth *are* perfect and superwhite like the stars' teeth in *People* magazine.

"They look really nice," I say with as much enthusiasm as I can work up. I run my tongue across my front tooth that overlaps the one next to it. But Roxie doesn't see the point of getting a mouthful of braces for one tooth. And until now, I didn't either.

"Thanks," Abigail says.

I point to her retainer. "How come you didn't tell me you were finished with that thing?"

"I didn't know until my appointment yesterday. I was going to tell you last night when we were on the phone; but the baby started crying, and you had to go take care of her."

"Oh." A sensation rises inside me that I've never felt about her before: big, fat jealousy.

Abigail's always been such a good friend, but suddenly I want things to be the way they were. Me hiding my secret behind my plain self and her with the frog face that kept the boys away. But now the frog face is gone and pretty soon Abigail will be, too.

"Maggie, I have to tell you something." Abigail is looking at me with anticipation in her eyes. It's the first time I've noticed how big they are; and now I can see that she's wearing shadow and liner, hardly noticeable, but it's there and it's working.

"What?" I haven't a clue where this is leading.

"You have to promise not to tell." Oh, boy. When a promise is involved, things are usually really good or really bad.

"Who would I tell?"

"I don't know. Lester, maybe."

I give her a get-real look.

"Okay. Here goes. I have a crush on a guy in school."

"Really? Who?" With her new look, whoever he is shouldn't be very hard to get.

"That new boy. He's so cute."

"What new boy?"

"Jacob Hauser. I saw him after my dentist appointment yesterday."

My heart drops to the floor. "You did? Where?"

"He was waiting for his mother in the office."

"His mother wears braces?"

"No. My dentist introduced me to her. She's an orthodontist. She just joined the practice."

"Oh."

"My mother told me that Jacob's parents got divorced, and I guess his mother has relatives here."

"Oh."

"And get this. His father's a rabbi. I didn't think rabbis could get divorced."

"How does your mother know all that?" I ask.

"I don't know. Maybe she heard it in the faculty room."

That could be.

"Anyway, when I was leaving, Jacob smiled at me and said hi." She stands up, walks over to the mirror, and piles her hair on top of her head the formal way. "I'm thinking of asking him to the dance."

"Oh."

"He's way too shy to ask me." The excitement in her voice is so strong it could be a live thing.

My insides have completely collapsed. I try to keep my face blank, don't let on that I feel like hurling my lunch. "I didn't think you wanted to go to the dance."

"I didn't." She picks up her retainer and scowls at it. "But then I got rid of this thing and started thinking that it might be fun."

"Oh."

"And I bet he wants to go, but he's too bashful to ask anybody."

"Oh."

"Maggie, you don't seem very excited. All you keep saying is oh."

"Sorry. I'm excited for you. I really am. I'm just surprised is all."

"You know what?" Abigail says.

"What?"

"I think I'll call him right now before I lose my nerve."

I need to get out of here. "Well, I guess I'll go home and give you some privacy."

Abigail grabs my arm. "Stay! I need moral support."

"But don't you want to be alone?" *I* do.

"No, I want you here. Then if he says yes, we can celebrate."

Oh, goody. That'll be a blast. "All right, I'll stay."

Abigail takes a sheet of paper off her nightstand, opens her cell, and dials the number she's written at the top. The rest of the page is covered with notes. She has obviously given this a lot of thought. "Hi, this is Abigail Flute. May I please speak with Jacob?"

A short pause.

"I'm fine. It was nice to meet you, too, Dr. Hauser."

Abigail covers the phone with her hand and whispers, "She's gone to get him."

I smile, but inside I feel like wringing her neck.

Abigail studies the paper. "Oh, hi, Jacob. This is Abigail Flute." She giggles. "But I guess your mother already told you that. I just called to see if you'd like to go to the school dance with me."

A long pause.

"Oh." Abigail's face has fallen. "Okay." She drops the paper into the wastebasket. "Yeah, right. See you in school."

She looks at me, doesn't say anything.

I look back. I don't say anything either.

This is awkward. Even though Abigail and I are best friends, we've only done homework together, gone to movies, or talked about everyday stuff, never anything as serious as boys. We are definitely late bloomers in the romance department.

"He said no." Abigail sounds defeated.

"That's too bad." I feel sorry for her. She must be so embarrassed. But I also feel like yelling YIPPEE!

"He said he was going to the dance alone and that he'd see me there."

My heart does a tiny somersault. Is there hope for *me*? "So, are you going to go?"

Abigail's face comes alive again. "You know, I think I will. Maybe he really does like me, but he's too afraid to go on a real date."

"Yeah," I say, pretending to be happy. "That *has* to be it."

Maybe I am in hell and just don't know it.

"I'd like you to meet Alexandra," Dr. Scott says as soon as he starts the group therapy session. "She'll be joining us for a few weeks." He's talking about me, and I love the way my beautiful fake name sounds when it comes out of his mouth. I offer the people a straight-line smile but don't say anything.

There are six of us sitting in a circle in what must have once been a fancy living room before Dr. Scott moved in. Now there are only mismatched folding chairs and a banged-up coffee table in the middle with a box of Kleenex on it. You can tell he is just starting out and is running his practice on a shoestring. If we were married, I could add the woman's touch: curtains at the windows and some put-together-yourself bookshelves from

Target to show off his college textbooks. And, of course, I would have his diplomas framed and hang them where all his patients could see them: right inside the office door.

I'm perched as close to Dr. Scott as possible, trying not to look as nervous as I feel. Meeting new people in a shrink's office is not something I'd sit up nights wishing for. He's dressed casual in jeans and a button-down shirt: light blue. His breath smells like coffee with extra cream and sugar.

A couple of people smile, and one man says hi, but the rest glare at me as if I've crashed their party. A girl about my age with bright-red hair stares at the clenched fists in her lap. Her legs are jiggling badly.

"Now, who wants to start?" Dr. Scott asks as he moves around on his chair to get comfortable then balances his notepad on his knee.

"*I* will!" calls out a skinny older woman who's been knitting since she sat down. "I didn't get much time last session." She gives the man who's sitting next to her a dirty look. "Some people seem to think their problems are more important than everybody else's."

"Go ahead, Gwen," Dr. Scott encourages. "What's on your mind today?" He sounds sincere, as if he really cares.

Gwen peers at him over old-lady half-glasses and licks her lips with the tip of her tongue, which darts in and out like a lizard before she says, "Same as always—those annoying telemarketers. They're ruining my life. I tell them I don't want what they're selling, but they won't give up. They just talk over me."

"So you're still having phone trouble," Dr. Scott interjects.

"Worse than ever," Gwen agrees. "If I'm not on hold to place my order from the shopping channel, it's those damn telemarketers." She lowers her head. "Excuse my French, but it upsets me that much. It's gotten so bad that just looking at the phone gives me hives."

A man across from her in a baseball hat yells, "For God's sake, woman, then don't look at it!"

Gwen's expression could shatter glass. "It's right *there* in my kitchen. How can I not look at it?"

The man takes in a huge gulp of air and lets it out slow. Then he continues at half speed, giving each word special attention. "Then move it or get yourself caller ID. If it comes up as 'unknown number,' ignore it."

"But it might be something I *do* want, and I'd miss out."

The guy grabs the cap off his head and smacks his leg with it as if he's trying to kill a cockroach. Then he looks at Dr. Scott and says, "Jeezum crow, Doc, she's hopeless. Can't you give us a little help here?"

Dr. Scott bites his lip as though stifling a smile. "Dan, I'm just the facilitator. I think you're doing fine."

Dan slaps his cap on his head and holds his hands in the air as if somebody's just told him to stick 'em up. "I'm finished," he says, defeated. "There are people here with real problems, and we're wasting time talking about a G.D. phone, for cripes sake."

"Thanks for not cursing, Dan," Dr. Scott says. He looks at

me. "That's one of our rules, that and not discussing politics or religion."

I nod as if I really care. I don't plan to say a word, so I won't be breaking any rules. Plus, Roxie's used every swear word that's ever been invented, so a little cursing wouldn't offend me.

"Any advice for Gwen?" Dr. Scott asks the group.

Everybody stays mute, looking everywhere but at Gwen. Dan's stone-facing the people as if he'll break anybody's neck who speaks up. The only movement in the room is that red-haired girl's legs, which are jiggling worse than before.

"Okay then," Dr. Scott says. "Who wants to go next?"

I pretty much tune out the whole thing and pretend that I'm listening while Dan talks about how afraid he is of feathers; and then a guy with a dragon tattoo on his neck drones on about his fear of throwing up, which is so bad he carries a plastic bucket everywhere he goes. This gives me the willies because it's right there on the floor next to him. But when he adds that he hasn't barfed since he was a kid, I forget about it and think how harmless their problems are compared to mine and that if we were playing loony bin poker, I'd go home rich.

"And how about you, Chloe?" Dr. Scott asks. He's talking to the red-headed girl. She's still looking down, but now she's holding her legs steady with her hands, her knuckles pure white from the force it's taking. This gets my attention. Things are about to get interesting. Nobody could be as wound-up scared as she is without something to show for it. "Do you have anything you want to share?" Dr. Scott adds.

She shrugs. "Just that the bad thoughts are still coming, and they're getting worse."

Now I'm really hooked, and I wonder how many people *she's* murdered. She has to be way deeper into the voices-in-her-head junk than I am. I try to act nonchalant, as if she's just another telemarketer-feather-puking phobic. But my heart is pounding bad—I'm not the only one after all.

"Worse how?" Dr. Scott probes.

Her legs are dancing again, and now she's picking at a hang-nail. "It's not just my father anymore. Now it's my mother, too." Boy, she is in deeper than I am. I can't imagine killing Roxie or Harry. "They're always on my case to do my homework," she continues, "so I'll get a scholarship and go to college to be a teacher. I hate kids, and my parents know I want to go to cosmetology school." She gives Dr. Scott a hopeless look. "I feel like cursing at both of them, slapping them, even."

Cursing and slapping? Is that all? I just hate it when you are ready for something good and then nothing.

"It's just that the Bible says I should honor my mother and father; and I'm afraid if I act out my bad thoughts, I'll go to hell."

If that's all it took, I'd already be the devil's assistant. But then I think of the monster in my head. Maybe I am in hell and just don't know it.

"Does anyone have advice for Chloe?" Dr. Scott asks.

The guy in my head would have some pretty good tips: incinerate them in the backyard or shove them off a cliff. She'll never have to do homework again, and she can spend the rest of her life washing people's filthy hair and waxing their you-know-whats.

While the rest of the group solves Chloe's life-or-death problem, I think there's no way I can sit through this again. Then I remember what Dr. Scott said: when I open up about what is bothering me, we could go back to individual sessions.

As soon as they're done with Chloe, Dr. Scott asks if anyone else would like the group's input.

I sure can't say *Well, you see; it's like this. I have a guy who's living rent-free in my head, and he enjoys getting me to kill people.* Instead, I raise my hand halfway, as if I'm too afraid to talk.

Dr. Scott smiles at me. "Go ahead," he says. "Tell us what's on your mind."

"Snakes," I say, not missing a beat. "It's snakes."

Would you like to go to the movies
next Saturday night?

*I*'m guarding the punch bowl so it doesn't get spiked and our school won't get sued by a bunch of angry parents like last year. I'm alone in the lobby just outside the gym, sitting at the refreshment table and watching a ball of pale-green foam that used to be lime sherbet float around the puddle of Hawaiian Punch and pineapple juice in the bottom of the bowl. And leave it to Roxie—she did find a poodle skirt and saddle shoes in the vintage shop, so I look like a moron. Plus, the pie she made is sitting there untouched amid the almost-empty plates of mini-sandwiches and broken cookies. The fact that the note I took home specifically asked for two dozen brownies didn't faze

Roxie one little bit. "This is a special occasion," she said, putting extra emphasis on the word *special* to make her point. "Brownies won't do, so I'm going to make your favorite: raisin pie."

Once Roxie gets something in her head, it's stuck there like cement, so I knew nothing I could say would change her mind. And it could have been worse. She could have baked a wedding cake like the one she learned how to make in the cake-decorating class she took when she thought an at-home cake-making business would be a good idea. But when she realized that people aren't inclined to buy their celebration goodies from a funeral parlor, she changed her mind and now uses her talent on three-tiered birthday cakes for Harry and me.

The dance is almost over, so pretty soon I'll be able to go home and put this whole miserable night behind me.

Abigail's in a crummy mood because Jacob hasn't asked her to dance, and he said "Thanks anyway" when she asked him. Plus, I think it's going to take a little time before the other boys get used to the butterfly she's become and forget about the frog face, because she told me that none of them has come anywhere near her.

Lester Pint asked me to dance, but when I told him I couldn't leave my post, he walked away hangdog style. I've peeked in the gym a few times to see if Jacob Hauser is dancing with anyone. But no, he's just sitting on the bleachers, looking adorable.

As I'm about to go look for Miss Hanson to see if it's okay if I wrap up the leftover goodies and dump the punch bowl, I see

Jacob watching me from the gym door. I didn't pay any attention to the music that's been wafting from the dance until now: Bobby Darin's "Dream Lover."

I try to look busy rearranging the punch bowl, but I notice how dry my mouth has suddenly become and wish that the dance could go on forever.

When Jacob starts walking in my direction, the Fleetwoods begin to sing "Come Softly to Me," and my heart plays a drum solo on my ribs.

"It's like an oven in there," he says when he reaches the table. "Do you mind if I sit out here with you?" His face is flushed, which makes his dark-green eyes stand out even more.

"Oh, sure," I say, too fast and too eager. Before I stop to think, I drag the folding chair that's next to me around to the front of the table. I can hardly believe what a dolt I am!

He carries it back to where it was. I love the fact that he just smells like clean clothes, no cologne like Lester, who douses himself with as much as he can whenever he goes somewhere special. "How about I help with the food?" Jacob asks. His teeth are so perfect, but then why wouldn't they be with a mother who specializes in that kind of thing?

"That'd be great. There's not much left, though, so business is slow."

"Yeah, I know. Everybody's using the water fountains in the locker rooms. What kind of pie is that?"

"I'm not really sure," I lie. I'm certainly not going to own up to the fact that my favorite kind of pie is raisin. I'm probably

60

the only kid in the universe who likes it. "I don't even know who brought it."

"Well, let's cut into it and see." He picks up Roxie's silver pie server, slices through the whipped cream, and says, "Oh, good! It's raisin. My favorite. Do you want a piece?"

"Sure," I say, fake-surprised. "It's my favorite, too. If I'd known that, I would have gotten into it earlier." I take paper plates and plastic forks out of the bag I put under the table and hand them to him.

ɼ ɼ ɼ

"Here . . . just a minute. Stay still," Jacob says, leaning toward me. Frank Sinatra's belting out "High Hopes," and Jacob and I are working on our second helpings of Roxie's masterpiece when he reaches over, runs his hand across my mouth, then licks his fingers. "You had some whipped cream on your lip."

Holy shit! My mouth germs are actually mixing with his. Then I close my eyes, try to slow my breathing. *Oh, please, God. Don't let Roxie's filthy words slip out of my mouth. I don't think Jews are allowed to swear.* I've never heard Harry curse even once. "Thanks," I say, touching my lips. I'm a little surprised they're actually still there. I thought they might have melted away under his warm, smooth touch.

"No problem," he says, smiling. "You don't want anything to spoil your perfect face. Did anybody ever tell you that you look like the girl in the J.Crew commercial?"

That girl's really pretty, but I guess we do have the same color hair and eyes. She even wears glasses like me. I look over to see if he's serious. His face says he is. "The J.Crew girl? Really?"

"She reminds me of you every time I see it."

The fact that Jacob Hauser is comparing me to one of the hottest girls ever makes me light-headed. I change the subject because being the center of attention is twisting my stomach into a knot. "So, how do you like Allenburg?" Well, that was lame, but it was the only thing I could think of to say.

"I like it better now," he says, looking straight at me.

*Dear sweet Jesus. He really likes me.*

If I acted the way I feel inside, I'd pounce on him and kiss him so hard and so long I'd be arrested for assault. Instead, I rein myself in and ask another boring question. "Where did you live before you moved here?"

"In Chicago." He smiles. And then he says, "Would you like to go to the movies next Saturday night?"

*Oh, my God! Thank you, Lord. I don't know what I did to deserve this, but I'll try to make it up to you. I might even start going to church.* "I'd love to. Which movie?"

"Doesn't matter to me."

"Me neither."

Dion starts to sing "A Teenager in Love."

"I like that song," Jacob says, almost in a whisper. I feel him staring at me, then watch as his hand moves toward mine.

My heart does a somersault. "I like it, too."

"I'll play it for you on my guitar someday," he says.

"You play guitar?"

"Yeah, I'm not any good, but it's fun."

I bet he's great and is just too modest to say so.

As I'm drowning in happiness, I look at the gym door and see Lester and Abigail glaring at me, and I feel a tiny bit guilty. Silence hangs in the air until Conway Twitty croons the first few notes of "It's Only Make Believe," and I have a feeling that something awful is on its way. But then I tell myself to cut it out. Good stuff can happen, too.

I look over at Jacob and think how sometimes life unfolds in your favor, and you don't know who to thank. But then I see Roxie's pie and think how important tonight was to her. And if she hadn't been her offbeat, pushy self, I wouldn't even be here.

It wasn't like that.

I t's the Monday after the dance, and I'm in the cafeteria when I see Abigail in the lunch line. She has a brown bag, so all she has to buy is something to drink and ice cream if she wants some. I'm sitting alone at a table in the corner where they store the chipped trays and bent silverware. I chose this spot because I'm not sure where Abigail will want to sit. Maybe with me—or maybe (now that she looks so cool) with the popular kids. But if she hasn't been accepted yet, she should have first dibs on the loser table without me there to interfere. You have to give a wronged person some consideration—especially if you are the one who wronged her.

Abigail walks toward the loser table and is nearly there when she spots me. I expect her to give me the cold shoulder like I would have done to her, but she doesn't. She heads straight in my direction, her eyes spitting fire. She sits exactly opposite me, says nothing, dumps her lunch bag on the table—wheat-bread sandwich, pickle, grapes—then opens her Snapple iced tea and takes a long drink.

She is not looking at me, and she is doing an excellent job of making me squirm.

"I'm really sorry," I say.

"For what?" Still no eye contact.

"You know."

"No, I don't." She is really making me work for this.

"The Jacob thing."

She puts down her iced tea and glares at me hard. "What was that all about, anyway? I went to the dance like an idiot because I thought maybe he liked me. You must have known all along that he didn't. How could you let me make a fool of myself like that? You even sat next to me when I called him. You must have known he was going to say no."

"It wasn't like that." I'm starting to feel desperate.

"Well, then what *was* it like?" Her tone is saying, "I'm through with you. I just need to tell you how I feel first."

"Before you invited him, I *was* hoping he would ask me. But when you called him, I thought he'd say yes." I look down at my hands, at the hangnail I've been fiddling with.

"So when *I* called him, you already liked him?"

"Yes. But then you asked him and he said no, so I figured I didn't have a chance."

"Why not?" Abigail unwraps her sandwich: egg salad, her favorite.

"Well, just look at you," I say, honestly. "If you were a guy, which of us would *you* choose?"

She shrugs. "You, I guess. That's what he did."

It amazes me that she really thinks that. "You have no idea, do you?"

She gives me a questioning look. "About what?"

"How pretty you are."

"Well, I'm better than I was, but you have all the important stuff."

I have no idea what she's talking about. "What stuff?"

"A personality."

"You have a *good* personality," I say. I'm being a little generous here, but I think Mrs. Flute's responsible for Abigail's blahness. And now that Abigail's pulling away from her mother, that could change pretty fast.

"No, I don't. I never know how to act around people." Now *she's* picking at a hangnail.

"Me neither," I add. This is not a lie. I am pure terrible at small talk. After I say 'Fine, thank you,' I don't know what to say next.

"Well, you seemed to know what to say to Jacob. You two looked pretty cozy."

I shrug. "We didn't really talk that much."

This is that iffy time when you don't know if a lie has worked. It could go either way.

"Did he ask you out on a date?"

Darn! I knew this was coming. "Just to the movies." I try to sound blasé, as if it's nothing.

"Well, *that's* a date!"

"I guess so, but it's not like a fancy dinner or anything like that." I am such a fake. I don't even believe myself.

This will be the end of the line for Abigail and me. I'm a dirty traitor. She'll never be able to trust me. I expect her to gather up her lunch and leave. Instead, she takes a big bite of sandwich and chews like crazy.

I'm not one bit hungry, but because I need to look busy, I do the same with my BLT.

"Maggie?" Abigail's finished her sandwich and is looking straight at me. Her face has changed to regular.

"What?"

"I know you didn't plan what happened with Jacob. I would have done the same if I'd had the chance."

Wow. I didn't expect that. I guess, like me, Abigail knows not to push too hard. When you have just one friend, you stay inside the safe zone so you don't end up eating lunch in the corner with only chipped trays and bent silverware to keep you company.

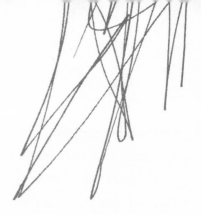

It's your funeral.

"Let's talk more about your fear of snakes," Dr. Scott says after we're settled in his office and he's finished with the usual niceties he always starts out with.

This is the first time I've seen him since the group session, and part of me is relieved to be away from the other people and to have him to myself again. There's this other part, though, that's super jittery about making the lie I told in group sound believable. Dr. Scott is a professional who has been trained to tell if people are yanking him around—like I've been doing since the very first day I started coming here. I Googled him; and his schools are Vanderbilt and Yale, so this man knows a thing or two.

"Okay," I say. "But I don't even like to talk about snakes." I press my hands together the prayer way and tuck them between my knees because I don't know what else to do with them. "I feel like such a coward."

"Fear of snakes is very common and nothing to be ashamed about," Dr. Scott says in a kind, patient way. "So I'm a little curious about why it took you so long to bring it up."

He is on to me for sure. I picture myself at home with Maud, her head in my lap. Something good on TV. I shrug. "I don't know. I guess I was just embarrassed."

"How about if we get back into your nightmares? Are they always about snakes?"

*Why do you tell a stranger your personal shit? He's just baiting you. It won't be long before you spill your guts and you'll be behind bars, same as your old man.*

What?!

*Just get up and leave. He can't make you stay.*

Oh, God. Not here. "Can we do this later?" I whisper to the man in my head. "I'm a little busy right now."

*Suit yourself. It's your funeral. I'm pretty sure they still have the death penalty in New York State. And, Maggie, you shouldn't take the Lord's name in vain.*

Oh, great. He's self-righteous on top of everything else.

"Maggie?" It's Dr. Scott.

So I don't have to look at him, I concentrate on the plant next to his chair: one of those tall, spiky ones that thrive even if you don't water it, which Dr. Scott doesn't, because the soil it's planted in is cracked dry.

"Maggie?" Dr. Scott is leaning forward in his chair. Worry lines have formed between his eyes—little railroad tracks.

"Yes?" I say, as busted as I feel. He'll probably ship me off to a mental institution. I'll never be able to slide what just happened by him.

"Who were you talking to?" Dr. Scott's tone is pure worried.

I shake my head and try to make my voice sound convincing. "Nobody. Well, sometimes I talk to myself. Does that mean I'm crazy?"

He sits back. His face has returned to semiregular. "No, but do you ever hear voices?"

"Sure. When people are talking to me." That sounded pretty sane.

"I don't mean then. Do you ever hear someone talking to you when you're alone?"

I fake a laugh. "No. Of course not. How could I hear someone talking if nobody's there?" I wish he wasn't so smart.

Dr. Scott jots one word on his notepad. I can't read what it says, but I watch him write a question mark after it.

"Did you just write that you think I might be nuts because you heard me talk to myself?" I ask.

"No. I wrote that you might have an attention problem because sometimes it seems hard for you to stay focused on our conversation."

Well, if you weren't so drop-dead gorgeous and I didn't have this jerk in my head who talks to me at the same time you do, maybe I wouldn't have an attention problem.

"Oh," I say.

"Okay. Let's get back to the snakes," he says, as if the craziness never happened. "Are they in your nightmares?"

"Yeah. Lots of them." There are never any snakes, just me killing people.

"Is the dream always the same?"

"Yes, always." It's never the same, but I'm always evil. In last night's nightmare, I killed Ali Rogers just the way the man told me to. When she hit the wall at the bottom of the stairs, there was nothing left but a huge blood spot in the shape of a baby, no sign of sweet little Ali. And when her mother came home, I beat *her* to death with the fig bowl.

"Tell me about this recurring dream." Dr. Scott has his pen ready. I picture him rubbing his hands together and thinking, *Well, finally I have a real nutcase on my hands. All those years in school weren't wasted after all.*

I scoot around in my chair a little, clear my throat. "When the nightmare begins, there are these little drawers in my mattress—lots of them, all sizes. There's a different kind of snake in every drawer, and they're all poisonous." I stop talking and start breathing hard, as if I'm too scared to go on.

"Have you always been afraid of snakes?" Dr. Scott asks. I can't tell by his voice if he's buying the story.

"As long as I can remember." I take in a big, shuddery breath and make my whole body shiver as I'm letting it out. Actually, I'm not one bit afraid of snakes. If Roxie wasn't so petrified of them, I'd have one for a pet. But then I think of Maud and realize that wouldn't work.

"Do you remember anything in your past that might have triggered this fear?"

"You think what happened when I was little might have something to do with it?" I ask, all phony-interested.

"Maybe. It's a possibility."

I screw my face around a little, stare at the ceiling, and sigh. Then I make a Eureka! expression. "When I was five or six, I was visiting my grandfather's farm. He and I were in the cornfield, and a black snake slid across my bare foot." I am such a moron. All Dr. Scott has to do is ask Roxie about my grandfather's farm to find out that neither of those things exists: one's fake and one's dead.

"How did you feel when that happened?"

"It freaked me out. And you know, come to think of it, it was my friend's grandfather, not mine. I never knew my grandfather, so I don't know if he had a farm or not." That should take care of it, but just to make sure, I add, "It's just that it happened so long ago; it's hard to remember."

Dr. Scott's cautious look has returned in full force. "Is that all there is to the nightmare or is there more?"

"Oh, there's more," I say, matter-of-fact. Now I have to think of something that would make a person scream bloody murder. . . . Okay, I've got it. "You see, there's this big black clock in my dream, the kind that chimes every fifteen minutes like in British movies. When it strikes twelve, all the snakes wake up and crawl through the mattress toward me. I'm so frozen with fear that I just lie there until I'm completely covered with a mass of knotted, wriggling snakes with their tongues darting in and out. That's when the screaming starts and I wake up." I'm kind of scaring myself. One snake is fine, but not a mountain of them. "And so do Roxie and Harry." I lower my head and try to force tears. My eyes do not cooperate, so I give up and look as sad as possible instead.

"Well, I can understand how frightening that is. It would even be disturbing to people who aren't afraid of snakes."

For goodness sake. I did it. He believes me. Sometimes you are so talented at a thing, you surprise yourself. He'll probably do that exposure therapy I read about when I looked up phobias. It'll be so easy for me. I'll be able to get rid of my so-called fear of snakes in a flash. He'll probably only want to see me half as often, which is fine with me now that I have Jacob. "Yeah, it is pretty scary," I say.

"Well, Maggie, I think we'll stop a little early today." He puts his notepad and pen on the table and pushes them to the far edge as though he won't need them again.

I doubt he'd cut a session short if he didn't think I was nearly cured. And this is extra good because Jacob is going to come to my swim practice, and we'll have some time to talk before it starts. "So when should I come back?" Probably once a month for a couple more times and then he'll release me.

"I'd like to see you again this Wednesday and then *every* week for a while. How does that sound?"

This is pure weird. "Okay, but why? Don't you think I'm getting better?"

Dr. Scott's face is straight-line serious. "We'll just have to keep digging until you decide to tell me what those nightmares are really about."

*    *    *

As I'm getting ready for bed, Dr. Scott's worried face enters my head, and I know there's no way I'll ever be able to tell him the truth. Then I think of Jacob and how sweet he was at swim practice. But things will never work out with us. The evil I've done has already started to catch up with me. The lead story on tonight's six-o'clock news was about the body two hikers discovered at the base of Sullivan's Mountain. They didn't give any details, but I bet when they do their investigation, they'll find my DNA on the back of his shirt, just like the forensic experts do on TV.

I peer out the window and watch lightning paint white streaks on the dark sky and listen as thunder mumbles in the distance. While I'm getting into bed, I think about myself and how much a person's life can change in such a short time and how tired I am. Just as I start to think about the hole that's where my heart used to be, Maud's snoring turns into a lullaby, and the sweet mystery of sleep steals me away.

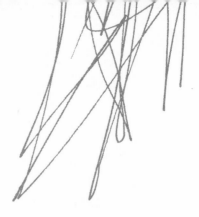

# Do you plan to kiss Mary-Magdalene?

"Where's Harry?" I ask Roxie when I get home from school. "He said he'd help me study for my biology test."

"He's embalming Mr. Sullivan." Roxie's in the living room polishing the leaves of her plants with mayonnaise.

"Mr. Sullivan?" My heart beats double time. This can't be happening.

"The man they found in the woods. You know. We saw the story on last night's news."

Sometimes a thing happens that stuns you so much, you actually are speechless.

"You remember," Roxie says as I stand there gawking at her. "When nobody came forward to claim the body, I figured

75

we could provide a funeral and a decent burial. It's the least we can do."

What does she mean by "the least we can do"? She must know. Oh, my God, she knows. But how?

"For heaven's sake," she continues. "The man's lived in the area his whole life. His relatives took the fortune the state paid for the land that was partly his and moved south, left him penniless—just because he was an alcoholic. The only thing he got out of it was the right to live there until his death. It doesn't seem fair. They could have used some of that money to send him to rehab instead of abandoning him."

Nothing from me. Relief inside, though.

Roxie stops polishing and points the mayonnaise rag at me. "I just remembered. You and Lester went hiking on Sullivan's Mountain a little over a week ago. Did you see Mr. Sullivan when you were there?"

Still mute.

"He must have been real fond of animals, living in the woods and all. I just thought he might have seen Maud. He would have loved her. She's so cute."

I have to be careful here because Roxie might ask Lester the same question. "Actually, we did see him, but he was in a bad mood, so he didn't say anything about how cute Maud is." I don't mention the gun part because that would freak Roxie out, and there'd be a bunch more questions. Besides, Lester hasn't spoken to me since the dance, so Roxie's not likely to see him anytime soon.

"Mr. Sullivan had probably been drinking," Roxie says. "He sure was the day he fell off the mountain. The death certificate says that alcohol was the cause of the accident."

There's still a tiny bit of worry inside me. "Does the death certificate say when he died?"

"The expert they called in said a little over a week ago." Roxie stops and looks as though she's calculating something in her head. "I wonder if I should tell the coroner that you saw him alive when you were on Sullivan's Mountain."

If I say not to, she will.

She sighs hugely, then waves her hand in the air as if she's dismissing the idea. "What's the point? It would just be more work for him. What's done is done."

*You lucked out on that one.* The man in my head can't mind his own business. He and Roxie would make a good pair. In fact, maybe they did at one time. I wonder again what Lonnie Kraft's voice sounds like.

*Did you hear me? I said you lucked out on that one.*

It's gotten so that sometimes he expects me to answer him out loud, as if he wants me to know that he's the boss.

"I heard you," I whisper.

Roxie looks at me funny. "What did you just say?"

"I said I think it's nice of you and Harry to provide the funeral." This is not the first time they've done that, and I really do think it's generous of them.

"Why were you talking so low? Are you getting a sore throat?"

"No, I'm fine. I was using a funeral voice. You know, out of respect for Mr. Sullivan."

I don't know if Roxie bought that or not, but she changes the subject. "A boy named Jacob called just before you got home. He wants you to call him back."

A little zing in my heart. "Oh, okay. Thanks." I turn to leave.

Roxie grabs my hand. "Well?"

"Well what?"

"Who is he?"

"Just a boy from school." I know if I say any more, she'll get all weird and pepper me with questions. I haven't even told her that I'm going to the movies with him.

I try to leave again, but now she's gripping my wrist so I can't get away. "So tell me more about this Jacob boy."

"What do you want to know?"

"Well, for starters, why he's calling you?"

"He probably just wants to talk."

"Talk about what? You never mentioned him before."

Oh, shoot. I might as well just tell her. She's going to find out soon enough anyway.

"He asked me to go to the movies with him. On Saturday."

Instead of doing cartwheels like I thought she would, she gets all busy around the eyes, and her mouth tightens. "So when did all *this* happen?"

"At the dance."

"You told me that you didn't dance with anybody."

"I didn't."

"Well, then how—"

"He just came over to the refreshment table and asked me. What's the big deal?" Oh, boy. I wish I hadn't said that. I know better than to sass her when her face is twisted into a knot.

"The big deal is that your father and I don't even know this boy. He could be . . ."

I bet she was going to say "just like that bastard Lonnie Kraft."

"He's nice, Roxie. You'll like him."

"Well, you're not going anywhere with him until we meet him." Her eyes are darting back and forth as if she's watching a tennis match. "You tell him that when you call him back."

Oh, for crying out loud. "We're just going to the movies."

"A lot can happen at the movies." Her neck turns a splotchy pink, and I wonder if that's where I was conceived—a *back-row baby.*

"I thought you *wanted* me to have a boyfriend," I say, half-way civil.

Her shoulders sag. "That's when you didn't have one." She looks me straight in the eye. "Mary-Magdalene, I'm glad you have a date. It's just that you're my baby girl, and I don't want anything bad to happen to you." Then she says exactly what I'm thinking. "I don't want you to get mixed up with a loser like I did."

"Jacob's not a loser, Roxie, but I'll see if he can come over."

*ı ı ı*

As I answer the door, Roxie's standing next to me. "Hi, Jacob," I say. "Thanks for coming."

"That's okay," he says, upbeat. "Thanks for asking." He looks at Roxie and smiles. She does not smile back; and before I can introduce them, she says, "You must be Jacob."

Oh, brother. This is going to be a disaster. At least I had a chance to warn Jacob about Roxie's quirkiness before he got here.

"Come upstairs to our apartment, Jacob," Roxie adds. "Mary-Magdalene's father would like to talk with you."

Darn! Now Jacob knows my stupid real name. He'll think I should be wearing a nun's habit and leave. But nope. He says, "Sure, Mrs. Feigenbaum. I'd like to meet Maggie's father."

When we get upstairs, Maud comes over to greet Jacob. He ignores her; and when she doesn't take the hint, he holds out his foot to keep her away. She tucks her tail between her legs tight then turns and goes back to wherever she came from. This is strange because she usually pesters visitors to death, demanding attention even from people who don't make a fuss over her.

"Don't you like dogs?" I ask Jacob.

"Dogs?" he says absentmindedly, as if he might be stalling for time.

"Don't you like them?"

"Oh, sure," he says. "They're okay."

This surprises me, but not everybody is as crazy about animals as I am. I guess he's allowed to have one flaw.

Harry's standing at the island in the middle of the kitchen, making a peanut butter sandwich. When he sees Jacob, he puts down the knife and holds out his hand. "Hey, Jacob. I'm Harry. Nice to meet you."

"Nice to meet you, too, Mr. Feigenbaum," Jacob says as he shakes Harry's hand. Jacob's wearing a light-blue T-shirt that makes the tan skin on his arm even more noticeable, his arm that is so masculine I can hardly stand it: all bones and tendons and angles.

"Anybody want a sandwich?" Harry asks us.

Roxie and I both say no thanks, but Jacob says, "Sure. That'd be great." Harry opens the bread package, starts to take some out. "I can make my own," Jacob says. "You go ahead and eat yours."

"Sounds like a plan," Harry says as he's sliding the bread and peanut butter toward Jacob.

Roxie and I sit next to each other on the stools and watch. She pours herself a cup of coffee. I'm waiting for her to give Jacob whatever little speech she has prepared to scare the bejesus out of him.

"I hear you're taking our daughter to the movies on Saturday," Harry says after he's downed the first half of his sandwich. Now I see. Roxie has designated Harry to do her dirty work.

"That's right," Jacob answers. "If it's okay with you and Mrs. Feigenbaum."

"Well, that depends," Harry says, serious. There's still the usual smile in his eyes, though.

Jacob stops spreading peanut butter. "On what?"

81

"If you pass the test or not."

"Test?"

Harry takes a piece of paper from his pocket, unfolds it, places it on the counter. There's a long list in Roxie's handwriting. He looks at Jacob's bewildered face. "Ready?"

"I guess so." I just know that Jacob is thinking that I am *so* not worth this.

"Okay, here goes," Harry says, official-like. "What's your full name?"

Jacob looks at me with a question mark on his face.

I shrug, wishing there were a hole I could crawl into.

"Jacob Mark Hauser."

"Address?"

"Sixty-eight Palmer Street."

"Phone number?"

"689-4112."

"Contact person?"

"Miranda Hauser."

"Her phone number?"

"Work or home?"

"Both."

"Work is 689-0598. Home is 689-4112."

"What are you going to do after you finish high school?"

"Become a rabbi."

Harry tries to hold back a smile; he doesn't. Roxie chokes on her coffee. If I were drinking anything, I'd choke, too.

Harry continues. "What movie are you taking our daughter to?"

"*Toy Story 3.*" Jacob thought fast on that one. We still haven't decided on the movie.

"How are you going to get there and back?"

"My mother said she'll drive us." Oh, good. That means Roxie won't be making a spectacle of herself in the convertible.

Harry turns his hands palm side out. "That's it," he says—satisfied, I think, that he's done his part.

Roxie scowls then taps the paper with her forefinger. "You forgot this one . . . and this one."

Harry gives her a puh-leeze look but continues his assignment. "Where will you sit in the movie theater?"

"I don't know." Jacob looks at me. "Where do you want to sit?"

In the back row so we can make out. "The middle, I guess."

"The middle," Jacob says.

"Okay, last question." Harry reads it to himself then shakes his head and slides the paper over to Roxie. "You'll have to do this one. I'm going to finish my sandwich."

I look over and see 'Do you plan to kiss Mary-Magdalene?' I guess Roxie realizes how ridiculous it is because she grabs the paper, crumples it, drops it into the wastebasket, finishes the last of her coffee, and leaves.

"I think you passed," Harry says to Jacob as he's patting

him on the shoulder. Then Harry laughs. "You sure are a quick thinker. I never could have done that well."

As I watch Harry and Jacob down their sandwiches and then dive into a package of Oreos, I think what just happened was really kind of sweet of Roxie. I bet she wishes her parents had asked Lonnie Kraft the same questions.

*  *  *

"I'm sorry you had to go through all that," I tell Jacob as I'm walking him to the door.

"That's okay," he says with a smile. "You're worth it. Plus, how many guys get to take a saint to the movies? See you tomorrow, Mary-Magdalene."

I start to close the door but then he opens it again. "And you know that last question? The one your mother didn't ask?"

"Yeah?"

"My answer would have been yes."

## Seems fishy to me.

It's Wednesday morning and I'm just about to leave for school, but instead of heading out the back door like I usually do, I walk toward the viewing rooms at the front of the funeral parlor. The nameplate outside room B reads PATRICK M. SULLIVAN.

A lump comes into my throat that's so huge, I feel as if I'm being strangled. Then a mysterious force leads me into the room and over to the closed casket that's covered with a blanket of red roses, the ones I'd heard Roxie ordering yesterday. All I can think of is, What does the *M* in his name stand for? That and the fact that he was once an innocent little baby whose mother looked down at his tiny face and gave him an Irish first name to match the last. I bet his middle name is Michael. That would go well with the rest. And I bet his mother loved him and had high hopes that he'd live a long, happy life and die a peaceful death, in his sleep maybe, instead of being pushed off a cliff by a girl who has an empty space where her heart should be.

*He deserved what he got,* the voice in my head says. *You know you had to do it.*

"Shut up," I say. "Just shut up!"

Silence from him.

*ı ı ı*

A note from Lester falls to the floor when I open my locker. It's not a poem this time, just regular words scribbled on a scrap of lined paper:

> *I saw in the newspaper that you have a guest at your house.*
> *The article mentioned that the Walmart bag we saw*
> *Mr. Sullivan carrying was at the edge of the cliff. You told*
> *me there was no sign of him when you went up to get*
> *your phone. Seems fishy to me.*

I crumple the paper and put it in my pocket. As I'm closing my locker, my hands are shaking so badly, I drop the books I'm holding.

Lester must have been watching me because he appears from nowhere and says, "Here, let me help you with those." He picks up my stuff, smiles with just half of his mouth, and says, "You seem a little nervous. Are you okay?"

"Yeah," I say, plain. "I'm fine."

"Good. Well, have a nice day." And then he's gone.

I go in the girls' bathroom and flush the note down the toilet. As I'm leaving, I see my face in the mirror. It's as white as the blouse I'm wearing.

ɪ ɪ ɪ

When I get home from school, I notice Patty-Ann Thurston's adult tricycle parked next to the funeral home entrance. This surprises me because she usually stays downtown or on the road by the river near her trailer.

Curiosity takes me in the front door, which is a mistake because Mr. Sullivan's funeral is about to begin. As I'm passing room B, I look in and see that Roxie has rows of folding chairs set up for a crowd. Patty-Ann is sitting in the middle of the front row. The rest of the chairs are empty.

Before I can escape, Roxie grabs me by the arm. "Oh, good," she says. "I need you to stay for Mr. Sullivan's funeral. Harry's spent a lot of time planning the service, and nobody showed up."

I've spent the entire day worrying that Lester's going to rat me out. I'm not about to sit through a funeral for the man I murdered.

"I can't," I plead. "I have homework and then I have to go see Dr. Scott."

"It won't take long," she adds as she's ushering me into the room. "Do it for Harry." I hate when she uses the guilt-trip ploy. She knows I'd do anything for Harry. I give her a please-don't-make-me-do-this look. It doesn't work. She just smiles and heads toward the office to get him.

I sit next to Patty-Ann. She gives me a huge, toothless smile. Her salt-and-pepper hair is pulled back into a low ponytail and anchored with a hot-pink scrunchie that matches her high-top sneakers—no laces. The in-between stuff is a combination of plaids, prints, stripes, and polka dots with a wide white belt holding the whole mess together. It's as though she's wearing all the clothes she owns so nobody'll steal them while she's away from home.

*ı ı ı*

The priest Harry hired rambles on about the great hereafter and how Mr. Sullivan is in a better place. I'm hardly listening until he says, "We can all be comforted by the fact that Patrick Sullivan has been reunited with his wife, Helen, and baby daughter, Viola, whom he worshipped more than life itself."

Wife?! Baby daughter?! What horrible thing happened to them? No wonder he was such a creep. No wonder he was an alcoholic. No wonder he was mad at the world. I killed a man who was once a loving husband and devoted father. I want to get up and run as far away as possible, but the misery in my heart weighs me down like an anchor.

After the service Roxie turns to Patty-Ann and says, "Was Mr. Sullivan a friend of yours?"

"Not really," Patty-Ann answers. "I just knew him from school. The kids teased him awful because he was backwoods and brought squirrel sandwiches in his lunch bucket. He was always nice to me. I just came to thank him for that."

*　*　*

Dr. Scott's sitting there, waiting for me to say something. It seems like an eternity since he asked me why I look so down, and I told him I didn't want to discuss it and clammed up. All I can think about are ways to put an end to the pain I'm in. But thinking you can do something and doing it are two different things.

"Did something happen in school?" Dr. Scott wonders. I guess he can't stand the silence any longer.

"No, school was fine."

"A problem with your parents?"

I shake my head.

"Did you have a disagreement with one of your friends?"

"No."

"More nightmares?"

"Uh-uh."

"Well, Maggie," Dr. Scott says when he runs out of possibilities, "I think maybe we should stop for now." He reaches over and pats my hand. "Everybody has a bad day once in a while. I'm sure next time will be better."

"Dr. Scott?" I say.

"Yes?"

"Do you believe in heaven?"

He uncrosses his legs and then crosses them the other way. At first I think he's not going to answer me because I know talking about religion is forbidden in group, so maybe it is here, too. "What's *more* important, Maggie, is, do *you* believe in heaven?"

"I do," I say. "I do believe in heaven." I'm just sorry I won't be able to go there.

Dr. Scott smiles.

"And you know what else?" I add.

"What?"

"I believe when people die, they get reunited with the ones they love."

"I'm glad, Maggie," Dr. Scott says. "I'm glad that's what you believe."

But then Dr. Scott's face changes to concerned. "Why were you thinking about heaven?" He tries to make his voice sound regular, but there's something there.

Oh, now I see. He's wondering if I'm thinking about committing suicide.

"I just came from a funeral, and the preacher mentioned it, that's all."

Dr. Scott nods, seems satisfied with my answer.

"The funeral was for Mr. Sullivan, the man who fell off the mountain."

"I read about that in the paper. Did you know him well?"

"No. I didn't know him at all. It's just that there were all these chairs set up and nobody came to his funeral, so my mother asked me to stay."

"That was kind of you," Dr. Scott says, gentle. "I'm sure Mr. Sullivan would appreciate it."

A tear falls onto my cheek and more follow as I picture Mr. Sullivan hugging his wife and baby daughter. Then I watch as they walk through the clouds, all three dressed in white with huge, fluffy wings, heading toward the most brilliant light I've ever seen.

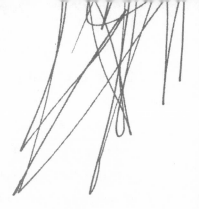

## What lighter?

It's the last day of school before summer vacation and tomorrow's my date with Jacob, so I'm in a great mood. Roxie says good things come in threes. I'm wondering what amazing surprise will come next.

The sun is shining, there's a little breeze, and a chorus of birds are singing. I'm walking to school empty-handed, no homework, because we just have to stop at the principal's office to pick up our report cards. I'm halfway there when Lester Pint catches up with me.

"Hi, Maggie," he says, bouncy, as though his silent treatment and the note about Mr. Sullivan never happened.

"What do you want, Lester?"

"Nothing," he says, all innocent. "Why do you think I want something? I just thought we could walk to school together."

I pick up speed. "I'd rather not, if you don't mind."

He matches my pace. "Well, I kind of do mind. You see, I have something I want to talk to you about."

My insides have twisted up good, but I try not to let on. The only thing he might want to talk about is the Walmart bag. But they must have thrown that away. Mr. Sullivan's death was ruled an accident. They don't keep evidence in a case like that. He's just trying to freak me out. I stop short, look him smack in the eye. "I don't have anything to say to you."

"You don't *have* to say anything. I'll do the talking."

Big man! "About what? That stupid Walmart bag? I told you Mr. Sullivan wasn't at the top of the mountain when I went up to get my phone. And neither was the Walmart bag. He must have taken it with him another day—the day he fell off the mountain because he was plastered. Now leave me alone!"

"You're right about the bag. He *could* have taken it another day."

"Well, then why are you acting like Encyclopedia Brown all of a sudden? Don't you have anything better to do?"

"I just wanted you to know—"

"I don't want to know anything. Now get away from me."

". . . that I have your mother's lighter."

I feel blood rushing to my head. "What lighter?" I know perfectly well what lighter, but how did *he* get it?

"The one you dropped the night you killed my father."

"Are you crazy?"

"No," he says, irritated. "But I think *you* might be. I saw everything from my bedroom window. When the flames started, it was as bright as daylight. I could see you perfectly. And before they took the mess away, I picked through the ashes with a stick and found the lighter you used. I was real careful not to ruin any fingerprints. Your mother's initials are R. P. F. Am I right?"

Roxanne Patricia Feigenbaum keeps repeating in my head.

"Well, am I?" Lester says. "I guess it wouldn't be very hard to find out. I could just ask her. And I bet she'd wonder why I want to know."

Sometimes a thing spooks you so much that your whole body shuts down. Your brain stops thinking, so you have nothing to say. The only thing you *can* do is stand there and hope you don't faint.

"Maggie," Lester says, "are you all right? You look terrible." His hand is on my arm, and I don't have the energy to shake it off.

I am concentrating on how his shirt is buttoned right up to the top like it always is. Now I'm studying the dark peach fuzz on his upper lip, which he should shave because it looks awful. Maybe when you haven't got a father to teach you, you don't know to do that. I can't look at his eyes, pale brown, almost colorless. I just can't because I would puke. "What are you going to do with it? The lighter?" The words sound as lily-livered as I feel.

"That depends on what you do."

"What do you mean?" This is all so strange. With Lester, I'm usually in charge. But now he has me cornered, like a cat about to pounce on a mouse. I don't know how to be the mouse with him.

"I owe you a lot for getting rid of my father," he says. "If you hadn't, I think my mother and I would both be dead. I assumed you did that because you loved me as much as I love you."

Well, you assumed wrong. "I thought I might someday. Why else would I do something like that? You were my friend. I couldn't stand that your father treated you like he did."

He looks at me as if I might actually be telling the truth. Not sure, though.

"This can all go away," Lester says, low. "Nothing bad has to happen to you."

"How? How can it go away?"

"I love you, Maggie. I love you more than anything. I just want us to be together."

I'd rather die. But wait! There might be a way out of this. I'm feeling more like the cat again.

"We've always been friends, Lester," I say, genuine. "And there was no reason my feelings couldn't go deeper"—I change my tone to hurt—"until you turned on me. I can't figure out why you did that." Although he's super book smart, he's pretty naive about regular stuff. "Why have you been so mean to me? I didn't do anything to you."

"You wouldn't go to the dance with me."

"I couldn't. I had to do the refreshments. I told you that."

"But what about that Jacob guy? Why was he at the table with you?"

"I don't know. I sure didn't invite him. He said he was bored and asked if he could sit down."

"You *let* him."

"I don't own the chair. There wasn't anything I could do. Besides, he was only there a few minutes."

"Well, you looked like you were having a good time. What were you two talking about?"

"I don't remember. How dorky the music was, I think. All I wanted to do was go home."

"Then why was he at your house the other day? And at your swim practice?"

My God. The little creep is stalking me.

"He came to my house to ask me to go to the movies with him."

"Are you gonna go?"

"No! I hardly know him."

"And what about swim practice?"

"I can't say who can watch and who can't."

"But you were talking to him . . . for a long time."

"He was asking me a slew of questions about our school. I guess it's a lot bigger than his old one." I make my voice sound serious. "To tell you the truth, I'm getting pretty creeped out by him. It's like he's stalking me or something."

Bingo! Lester's expression has changed to regular. "So you don't even like him?"

"Of course not! I mean, I don't hate him. I felt kind of sorry for him at first because he was new and didn't have any friends; but then he got weird, and now I don't want anything to do with him."

"I was wondering what you saw in him. He's so skinny, and his hair's all curly like a girl's."

I love Jacob's curly hair! "Yeah, he is pretty homely." He is so cute I can hardly stand it.

Lester's face says he's buying it. But what am I going to do when I get to school and Jacob's waiting for me like he said he would when we talked on the phone last night?

"Lester?" I say, kind of sexy-like. "Would you do me a huge favor?"

"What?"

"Will you pick up my report card so I don't have to run into that Jacob guy?"

"Okay, but what'll I tell the secretary?"

"Just tell her I'm sick, and I asked you to bring it home for me. If she says no, she can call my house, and my mother'll tell her it's okay." People tell me all the time that I sound just like Roxie, so that won't be a problem.

"But how am I going to get it to you?" He points up the street toward my house. "I'm not going in *that* place." Just what I was hoping he'd say.

"Is it all right if I come to your house this afternoon and pick it up?" I ask.

"Sure. That'd be great."

"And boy, is it ever hot. Do you think I could go in your pool? Will that be all right with your mother?"

"My mother's going to Albany for the day to shop or something, but she won't care if you swim. I'll just watch." I feel sorry for Lester. He told me once how his father used to hold his head underwater when he was teaching him how to swim. And that he called Lester a sissy because he cried.

"I don't want to swim alone," I say like we're friends again. "How about if I teach you? You don't even have to get your face wet. I'll hold on to you so you don't sink." That should do it.

"Maybe. We'll see."

"Okay, I'll bring my bathing suit just in case."

After the school secretary calls, I lie on my bed and go over my plan to get the lighter back. Pretending to love Lester isn't going to be easy. And the thought of kissing him instead of Jacob turns my stomach. But I'm sure he has Roxie's lighter in his room. I just have to convince him that I love him as much as he loves me so he'll give it back. I know this makes me a double-crossing sleaze, but the only other way to get that lighter would be to kill Lester. And I could never do that.

Kill him!

As I'm walking to Lester's, I think about all the times I've been at his house and the fun we had before we grew up and he started acting like he owns me. When his father was alive, we spent most of our time in Lester's room watching TV or playing video games or messing around on his keyboard to keep out of Mr. Pint's range of fire.

When I get there, Lester's sitting on the front step, reading a book. His house is so beautiful: old brick, cream trim, black roof and shutters, and a bay window with real copper splaying out over it like an umbrella. "Hey, Lester," I say happy, as though I'm just coming to watch TV.

He stands up, holds out my report card. "Here it is," he says, less excited than I thought he'd be.

A sinking feeling comes over me when I realize that he might have seen through my act and isn't going to be played for a fool.

"Thanks," I say. I can't tell if he's about to ask me if I want to swim or do anything else for that matter. I stall for time by opening my report card and studying it as though it's written in code. Maybe if I make him feel superior, he'll bite. "Oh, brother," I say, disgusted. "My mother is not going to be happy when she sees my math grade" Roxie never makes a fuss about math because everything else is A or A plus, which she told me she never got even once.

"What is it?" he asks. I knew he'd be dying to know.

"D," I say as though it tastes sour. Then I hang my head as if I'm a failure, someone to be pitied.

"Really?" he says as if he can't believe it. This is the first time I've ever told Lester how totally hopeless I am in math, but I think I'm on the right track here. He steps toward me, looks over my shoulder at the card. "Wow" is all he says, but he leans in closer. Can he smell the Vera Wang cologne I borrowed from Roxie's room? "Have you always been this bad in math?"

"Not till high school," I say. "This harder stuff just doesn't make sense to me."

"The concepts are really simple," he says, haughty. "*I* can show you how to do it." Good. He thinks he's the cat again.

"That'd be great. Thanks." I pretend to lose my balance, fall toward him. Our arms touch. A little of our fronts, too. "Oh, sorry," I say. I look down at my sandals. "These are new, and I'm not used to them yet."

"It's okay." His face has turned the slightest shade of pink.

I back up a few steps. "Well, I guess I'll go face the music. Might as well show the D to my mother and get it over with."

"I thought you wanted to swim." Exactly what I want to hear. My plan might work after all.

"Well, I did wear my suit, but I wasn't sure if you were busy or something."

"I'm not doing anything. I don't want to go in the water, though."

"That's no problem. Are you sure it's okay if I do?"

"Yeah, it's fine. I'll just watch." Right. Like at swim meets when he ogles me.

"Thanks," I say. "It'll feel great. I'm steaming hot."

"Yup, it's a scorcher."

"And after I swim, maybe we can go up to your room and play video games like we used to do."

Lester's look turns suspicious. He stares deep into my eyes as though he's trying to read my true thoughts. I stare back—don't look down, because if I do, he'll know for sure what I'm up to. "We'll see," he says with authority in his voice.

What's the matter with me? Have I blown this? I never should have mentioned going to his room. Too obvious. He'll guess I'm after the lighter. I have to try to fix things, so I look up at the clear blue sky. "On second thought, it's way too nice to spend it inside. I'd love to stay in the pool for hours—if it's okay with you."

"It's fine with me," Lester says. "Besides, my mother doesn't want me to have people in the house when she's not home."

He's lying. I'm his only *people*, and I've been in his house plenty of times when Mrs. Pint wasn't there. Instead of calling him on it like I normally would, I continue my mouse act and point to the gate that opens to the backyard. "Well, let's go then. I can't wait to jump in!"

*  *  *

This pool is so beautiful; it's like the ones you see in decorating magazines. It's surrounded by a wide brick patio finished off with fancy outdoor furniture. I take off my shorts and T-shirt, put them on the chair next to the one Lester's sitting on. Just like at swim meets, his eyes are glued to my chest, only this time he's getting a much better look because instead of a Speedo tank, I'm wearing my flame-red bikini with the halter top. And even though I'm regular from the neck up, I'm an A plus as far as the rest, thanks to Roxie's genes. I have a feeling it's not going to take very long for Lester to give up the lighter.

As I'm walking down the pool steps, I look over at him and say, "Do you think your mother would like to swim with me? The water's perfect." I know he said she was going to be gone, but I want to make sure. I certainly can't act all sexy and flirty in front of Mrs. Pint.

"No. Remember I told you she went to Albany?"

102

"Oh, that's right. I forgot." Good. I'll have all afternoon to work on him.

This pool is almost as big as the one at school. I slide into the water and head for the deep end, then float on my back so Lester can get a good look. Let him think that playing video games in his room might be a good idea after all. I have to let *him* make the first move, though.

I stay at the deep end on purpose and practice my strokes. I don't want Lester to think I'm here for anything more than swimming. Just as I'm about to climb out to show off on the diving board, Lester calls, "Maggie, how hard is that thing you were just doing?"

"What thing?"

"Where you were staying in one place with your head up."

"Oh, I was just treading water. It's really easy. It's what people do when they're tired or until they get rescued. You know, like in the movies when a boat capsizes. You could do it forever."

"Can you teach me that?"

"Sure. No problem."

"Will you hold on to me the whole time?"

"Of course."

"I'll be right back," he says. "I have to get some shorts." Poor Lester. He doesn't even have a bathing suit. I feel awful about tricking him, but I can't think of any other way. He could send me to prison with that lighter or blackmail me for the rest of my life. More important to me right now, he could make me cancel tomorrow night's date with Jacob.

Lester's standing in the shallow end of the pool, holding both my hands. He's so petrified that even being two inches from my front does nothing to lessen his fear.

"Walk around a little to get used to the water," I say, patient. I'm remembering my swimming lessons from when I was small. "Now move your hands back and forth just under the water like this, as if you're waving flies away. We'll only go out as far as your shoulders. You don't have to get your head wet, but you need enough water so you can kick your feet."

"Don't let go!" Lester says, holding my hands so tight, I'm losing circulation.

"I won't," I say. "Now stand still. And I'm right here."

Lester calms down a little and lets go of my hands.

"See? There's nothing scary about it. It's like standing in a deep puddle." I sound like a kindergarten teacher.

"You're right. It isn't that scary."

"Now we have to go out a few more inches so I can show you how to tread water."

Lester starts to back up. "I changed my mind," he says, low. "I don't want to do this. Maybe some other time. I'll just get out and watch you."

Pain stabs me in the temple, and at the same time the voice yells in my head. *You know what you have to do. Grab him! Pull him into the deep end.*

Lester turns and starts back toward the steps.

*I said, Grab him!* The voice is even louder now; my head is throbbing.

I do what he says, grab Lester, who loses his footing. I drag him into deeper water; and when he can't feel the bottom, he panics and latches on to my arm. I become a kindergarten teacher again. Gentle. Smiling. "Lester, relax. Just calm down and kick your feet like you're walking in place. I'll hold you up by the waist. You'll see how easy it is." While he's concentrating on that, I nudge him to the middle of the deep end. "Now shoo the flies away like I taught you. You're doing it. See? I told you it was easy."

"It is kind of easy, but stay next to me."

"I'm right here. Don't be scared. If you remain calm and keep doing that, you'll stay at the top. If you panic, you'll sink to the bottom and drown. Understand?"

He nods, keeps treading water.

I back away from him, make my voice blunt. "Where's the lighter, Lester?"

His eyes widen, and his look tells me he knows what's happening. "You're not going to leave me here, are you? I'll drown."

"No you won't. Not if you keep treading water." I remember his condescending remark about my math grade. "It's such a simple concept."

*Touché!* The guy in my head thinks he's a comedian.

"But what if I start to sink?"

"Then you *will* drown. Where's the lighter, Lester?"

"It's in my room," he gasps.

"Where in your room?"

"I can't remember. I'll have to look for it."

*Don't let him get away with that.*

"I won't!" I say to the voice. "Leave me alone. I can *do* this. Where's the lighter, Lester?"

I guess Lester figures he'd better hurry things along, because he says fast, "In the box my iPad came in."

"Where's that?"

"On my closet shelf behind the stack of DVDs," he pants. "But don't leave me here alone. I'll get it for you."

*You don't need him anymore. Do it now. It'll be a snap to drown that jerk. Nobody will ever know you were even here; it'll be the perfect crime.*

He's right. There are no other houses around. When the police investigate, they'll think it was an accident: Lester decided to go in the shallow end of the pool to cool off, and he walked out too far. And even if they find fingerprints or other signs that I was here, no problem. I've been at the Pints' house a million times.

*Kill him! Do it now!*

I am so tired of letting this thing in my head boss me around, but I start toward Lester; and as I do, I see the fear in his eyes. The same fear I used to see when his father shouted at him. Then I think of Mrs. Pint and how she's always been so nice to me and how much she loves her son. Worst of all is when I picture Harry's sad face. He would be so ashamed of me if I murdered the kid I grew up with. Harry's always liked Lester. I think he feels sorry for him, too.

*You have to do it!* the voice screams. *He'll never give the lighter back. He'll hold that thing over you forever.*

My head feels as if it's on fire. "I know!" I scream even louder. "Just let me think!"

Silence from the voice.

I swim to the bottom of the pool to calm down. My body relaxes as I admire the beautiful mosaic designs in the tile and run my finger along the edge of a huge golden fish with emerald-green eyes. Then I pretend *I'm* that golden fish and glide through the water until my thoughts clear and the headache lessens.

As I head toward the surface, I see Lester's live legs running in place. I think how easy it would be to pull them down. It would only take a few minutes, and I've heard that drowning isn't that bad: kind of like going to sleep.

But then I picture those legs—milk-white and stiff on the metal embalming table in our basement—and remember how afraid Lester is of the funeral home. Sometimes you just cannot do a thing, especially if it means you might end up in prison for the rest of your life and break your sweet stepfather's heart.

*ı ı ı*

Lester's still kicking and shooing flies like crazy when I get back with the lighter. He's in the exact spot he was in when I left. It amazes me that someone that smart didn't figure out that he could move in any direction and be out of the pool in a snap. Good thing brains and common sense don't always mix.

"Are you going to leave me here?" Lester asks, panting. "I can't do this treading-water thing much longer."

"Lester, do you remember this morning when you told me you loved me?"

"Yeah."

"Is it true?"

"Yes," he gasps, "you're the only kid my age who's ever been nice to me."

"If you love me, you wouldn't blackmail me."

"I couldn't think of any other way to keep you when that Jacob guy started moving in." He's breathing hard, and it's a struggle for him to get words out.

"You'll find a girl who will love you," I say. "It just won't be me. We can be friends, but that's all."

"Okay, but will you please get me out of here?"

"You can do that yourself. Instead of shooing flies, pretend you're pushing your way through the jungle."

Lester heads toward the shallow end. I wait until he can touch bottom. Then I grab my T-shirt and shorts and take off.

"Hey, Maggie," Lester yells after me. "Who were you screaming at in the pool?"

"Nobody," I call back. "You must have been hearing things."

*   *   *

When I get home, Harry's in viewing room A, getting ready to close a casket so he can take it to the cemetery. He leaves for a minute to answer the phone; and when he does, I tuck the plastic bag with the lighter down the side and into the bottom of the coffin. The occupant is a preacher's wife, and I doubt that she ever had a cigarette in her life. You never know, though—she might decide to take up smoking now that she's in heaven.

Before Harry returns, I run upstairs. The thought of what I almost did to Lester switches my stomach into reverse, and I head for the bathroom—fast.

When I'm finished, I lie on my bed and wonder how I'm going to get through the rest of my life. Just then Maud enters my room and whines for me to lift her onto the bed. I think about how innocent she is. And I know this sounds stupid, but I envy her for that. She curls up next to me, and I hug her like I used to hug my stuffed animals when *I* was little and innocent. "You're a good girl, Maud," I say. "Yes, you are—you're a very good girl."

Bite him!

*I*t's Saturday afternoon, and Abigail and I are in my room. She's helping me get ready for my date with Jacob. If there was a picture to go along with *loyal* in the dictionary, it would be Abigail. It's as if the tiff we had never happened, and she's actually happy for me. I wish I were like that. I am more the type to carry a grudge. It must be a lot easier on your insides to be the forgiving sort.

"What do you think about this outfit?" I say, turning around the *ta-da* way. I'm wearing my medium-blue jeans, short-sleeve print-over blouse, and dark-blue leather flip-flops.

"Perfect!" Abigail says. "Way better than the short skirt and low-necked tee." She looks at me, serious. "This is your first date, Maggie. You need to leave a little mystery, save the more revealing stuff for later." Even though Abigail has never had a date, she has a natural talent for style. That and the fact that she has a subscription to every teen magazine available make her the perfect fashion consultant.

I'm so new at this boy-girl stuff that if I'm not careful, I could follow Roxie down the floozy-fashion path. Lucky for me, I have Abigail to save me from myself in that department.

"How about if we do your hair next?"

"My hair?" I never even thought of changing my hair.

"Well, it's so long and shiny. We could just pouf it a little." She hesitates—maybe wondering if she's overstepped the boundary. "That's if you want to."

I'm not sure I want pouf, but I can undo it after she goes home. "Oh, I do," I say so I don't hurt her feelings.

"Good!" She goes over to the bed, opens her backpack, and takes out a round, bristly thing on a stick and a can of hair spray. "I'll use my thermal brush."

"When did you get that?" I ask. I've noticed them in stores, but I've never seen Abigail use one.

"This morning. You'd better sit down," she says. "I have something to tell you." She's smiling big like you do when a thing is so good you can hardly stand it.

I sit on the edge of my desk chair. "What? Tell me."

"Allison Jamison asked me to go to a party at her house next Friday." Allison Jamison is the head snot in the snotty girls' clique.

"Really?" I say, trying to sound thrilled for her. "When did *this* happen?"

"Last night. She called and asked me, just like that. She even seemed a little nervous."

"That's great! You're part of the in-crowd now," I say as enthused as I can manage. Even though I knew this was coming, I'm dying a little inside because I realize this is the beginning of the end for Abigail and me. I picture the *Titanic* right after it's hit that iceberg.

*, , ,*

"Hi, Dr. Hauser," I say after Jacob's introduced me to his mother. "It's nice to meet you." Jacob and I are sitting in the backseat of her Ford SUV. She's a classy-looking woman: short, dark-brown hair, green eyes like Jacob's, and thin like him, too. I look over at his lips—just the right amount of fullness—and can't wait to feel them on mine. Hope I do it right, though, because I'm sure it's not the same as practicing on my arm. I think of all the kids who make out in the halls at school and how good they are at it. I'm glad Jacob's shy and probably just as inexperienced as I am.

"How long have you lived in Allenburg?" Dr. Hauser asks me. She's just trying to make conversation, I think, because Jacob and I aren't saying anything to each other. It is hard to be anything but quiet with a mother right there.

"All my life," I answer. That always sounds so boring. I wish

I could say something like "Oh, just a couple of years. Before then I lived in Gay Paree."

"That's nice," Dr. Hauser says, polite.

"Yes, it is nice." I am so pathetic. A popular girl would make interesting conversation with her date's mother, not sit here like a ninny.

"It's a beautiful area with the lake and all," Dr. Hauser adds. She's trying to make her voice sound enthusiastic, but I think she's running out of steam.

"Yes, it is." I wish Jacob would help me here; but he seems preoccupied, just looking out the window, not smiling. I wonder what he's thinking about.

I guess his mother realizes how hard this is for me because she doesn't ask any more questions, and we finally get to the movies. Just before we get out, Dr. Hauser looks at Jacob, serious. "Remember what we talked about."

He gives her a look that could crack a rock.

She doesn't react, just says, "Call me as soon as the movie is over, and I'll come get you."

Darn! I was hoping Jacob and I would have more time together, maybe hang around the mall after the movie. His mother really keeps him on a short leash.

ɾ ɾ ɾ

"Do you want to sit in the middle?" I ask Jacob after we've entered theater 7 for *Toy Story 3*.

"There are a slew of kids down there," he says, annoyed. "The little jerks will blab all through the movie. Let's sit here." He reaches for my hand and leads me into the back row. I am going to get that kiss for sure.

"Your mother's nice," I say when we get settled in our seats. I know that's lame, but it's the only thing I can think of.

"What? Oh, yeah. She's real nice." There's an edge to his voice, but then he looks at me and smiles. "You're nice, too."

I giggle. "Thanks." I can't believe I said *thanks*. I am pure pathetic, and I hope he can't see how red my face must be.

Just then, as if God is giving me a present, the lights go down and the movie starts.

We finish our popcorn and Cokes. The previews end and the show starts. Jacob is glued to the movie, doesn't even hold my hand like at the dance. Maybe he just likes to sit in the back row or maybe he was serious about the kids in the middle making too much noise. And maybe he changed his mind about his answer to Roxie's kissing question.

Nope, I was wrong. He turns a little in his seat and puts his arm around me. He's going to kiss me soon, I think. And he does. It's nice, just what I'd been imagining it would be like. Then he kisses me again. Harder this time. Not so nice. Suddenly his tongue slithers into my mouth, slimy and wiggling. I picture an eel on the Discovery Channel, burrowing into the ocean floor. I pull away, wipe his spit off my mouth. Before I can tell him to cut it out, he grabs me, kisses me again; this time his hand slides under my blouse, and he's groping my breasts as if he's trying to decide which one he likes better.

"Cut it out!" I whisper, trying to pull his hand out from under my shirt. He's strong, though, and clearly has no intention of stopping, so I dig my fingernails into his skin. He relents. Before I know it, he squeezes the back of my head and kisses me so fiercely, my teeth sink into my lip. Now his other hand is fumbling with the button on my jeans.

So I do the only thing that will make him stop: Bite him! I clamp onto his tongue. He shoves me away. "Jesus Christ! Why'd you do that?" he whispers.

"Well, why'd you do what *you* did?"

"I thought you wanted it."

"Yeah, right. Like a bad case of the flu."

"Little girl, huh?"

I stand up, pull my shirt down, and push past him to the aisle.

He grabs my hand. "What are you going to do?"

I reach in my pocket for my phone. "Call my stepfather to come get me."

"Why?" He sounds a little desperate. "We were just having fun."

I taste blood from my lip. "That wasn't what *I* call fun."

I head for the theater door, welcome the lights in the hall. He follows me, says, "Oh, come on. I didn't mean anything. Let's go to the food court or the arcade."

"I'm not going anywhere with you." There's an empty feeling where all my hopes used to be. But I *am* glad that we were at the movies, where Jacob couldn't go any further. I bet I was his practice girl, so he'd be ready when he moves on to the popular ones. My mind goes back to his mother's car. I think about how she told him to remember what they talked about. It sounded like a warning. Maybe they didn't move to Allenburg so they could be closer to relatives. Maybe they moved here to escape the wrath of some other girl's family after she discovered what Jacob considers fun.

*ı ı ı*

"Are you sure he didn't do anything?" Roxie asks as we're walking into the kitchen.

Harry was out on a pickup when I called, so she had to come for me.

"I'm sure," I say, trying to make my words sound genuine. "I told you. I just don't feel well. I think I ate too much popcorn."

When she turns on the light, she zeroes in on my face, then runs her finger over my top lip. "What happened here?" It feels swollen inside, but I'm surprised it shows.

I think quickly. "Nothing really. The popcorn tasted so good and I was eating so fast that I bit my lip."

She nods as if she believes me. I know she doesn't.

"Do you want some ginger ale to settle your stomach?" Roxie asks. She's smoothing down my messed-up hair.

"No thanks. I think I'll just go to bed."

I start to walk away, but she takes hold of my arm, and I figure she's going to keep asking questions until I come clean. Instead, she cups my chin in her hand the way you'd hold a delicate robin's egg and says, "Mary-Magdalene, I'm glad you called. You did the right thing. You're a good girl. I'm proud of you."

As I'm heading to my room, my eyes well up. That's the first time Roxie's ever said she's proud of me. It makes me sad, though. She's proud of me because I'm not like her.

I undress and remember how much thought went into choosing these jeans and this blouse for my special date and how tomorrow I will take them to the Salvation Army and put them into the drop box out front. The bra, too, even though it's brand-new.

I hear Harry's voice in the kitchen and then Roxie's muffled whispers. Maud scratches the side of my bed. I lift her up, tuck her in tight next to me, and kiss her head. Tomorrow I will take her for a long walk, and she will flirt with Stanley, the Doberman, through the fence. He won't bark or growl or try to get at her. They will sniff each other's noses politely and leave it at that.

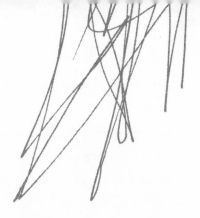

Guys expect more than just a kiss.

"Were you awake?" Abigail asks after I answer the phone at seven o'clock on Sunday morning.

"No, but I am now."

"How was it? Tell me everything." The excitement in Abigail's voice could generate electricity.

"There's not much to tell. We went to the movies."

"And . . . ?"

"And what? That's all. We went to the movies."

"Well, did you go anywhere afterward?"

"Home."

"That's it?"

"Yup."

"Did he like your outfit?"

I picture his fingerprints all over it. "He seemed to."

"What's that mean? Did he say anything about it?"

"Not really."

"What about your hair?"

"He didn't mention it." Just made a complete mess of it.

"Well, what did you two talk about?"

"Nothing much."

"Are you going out again?"

"No."

"Why not?"

"We just aren't."

"Did he ask you?"

"No."

"Oh." There's pity in her voice. "Well then, he'll probably call you."

"No, he won't."

Silence from her; but I bet she has her antennae in the air, and they're waving around like crazy. Finally she says, "Maggie, what happened last night? I mean really."

Silence from me now.

"What did *you* do to mess this up?" The old Abigail would have been on my side.

"*I* didn't do anything."

"Well then, what did *he* do?"

At first I'm not going to rat him out, but then I think, *Why not? He deserves it.* "He was all over me."

"What do you mean, 'all over you'?"

"He had his hands all over me."

"Jacob? But he's so sweet."

"That's what I thought, but he wouldn't stop."

"In the movie theater? With people all around?"

"*Yes.*"

"Where were you sitting?"

I was hoping she wouldn't ask me. "In the back row."

I can almost see Abigail's eyes rolling. "Well, no wonder. You *never* sit in the *back* row unless you mean business. It gives a guy permission to do whatever he wants. You have to set boundaries right from the start so he knows exactly how far he can go."

I shouldn't have told her. "That sounds like something you memorized from one of your teen magazines."

"Well, it wouldn't hurt *you* to start reading the dating advice columns. They're written by girls in the know. Whatever Jacob did isn't his fault. You gave him mixed signals."

"I didn't give him any kind of signals. I was hoping he'd kiss me, but that's all."

"Maggie, you're not in second grade. High school dating is serious business. Guys expect more than just a kiss."

"How would you know?" I say, defensive. "You've never even had a date."

"Not yet, but when I go to Allison's party, I'm certainly not going to get all prudish if a cute guy tries a few things. There are a lot of other girls out there, you know."

My blood is boiling. Even my ears feel hot. "Right" is all I can manage.

"Why don't you call Jacob and apologize for how you acted? Maybe he'll give you a second chance."

That does it. "Are you crazy? You think I should call and apologize to *him*? Not in a billion years."

"I didn't mean to make you mad. It's just that I hate to see you throw a perfectly nice guy away because he misunderstood what you wanted. If he accepts your apology, you can come over to my house, and we'll go through my magazines and give you a crash course in dating."

"That'd be great," I lie. "But I can't today. I promised my mother I'd help her polish the caskets in the display room. Maybe some other time."

"Oh, okay then." I think she's going to sign off, but instead she says, "Maggie, I just had a thought."

"What is it?"

"If it turns out that you're finished with Jacob, would it be okay if I ask him to go to Allison's party with me?"

I don't believe this. "It's okay, but you'd better watch out."

"You don't have to worry," she says, all confident.

I think about how fast she's changed, and it makes me sad. I picture the *Titanic* again, this time with one end sticking straight up, just before it sinks to the depths of the sea.

It'll be fun, just like bowling.

It's June 30th, my birthday: sweet sixteen. Roxie and Harry are going to take me out for dinner at Arnie's, my favorite Italian restaurant. When Roxie asked if I wanted to invite Abigail, I said she was sick and couldn't come. The truth is that we haven't spoken to each other since our phone conversation. The one time I saw her, she was with Jacob, and they looked very lovey-dovey.

"Ready to get your learner's permit?" Harry asks when I enter the kitchen. "After you pass the written test, we'll go out for a lesson."

"Sounds good to me," I say, putting an English muffin in the toaster. Harry's been taking me to practice in the parking lot

122

behind the school when nobody's there, so I already know a lot of stuff about driving.

He hasn't mentioned my date with Jacob because I think Roxie asked him not to. But today we're alone, and he's looking at me as though he's dying to say something.

I hurry it along. "What is it, Harry?"

The toaster pops up, and he snatches the muffin out. "Do you want butter and honey on this?"

"Sure, but I can do it."

"I'll do it. Just relax. I'll bring it over to you."

When he does, he sits on the stool next to mine, leans forward, and rests his arms on the breakfast bar. "You know, Mare, it's hard to tell about boys."

"What do you mean?"

"Well, take Jacob, for instance."

I'm just about to bite into the muffin but stop. "Okay."

"He came over here all clean-cut and polite. He knew exactly how to act and what to say to make your mother and me feel comfortable about letting you go out with him."

"I know."

"He sure had me fooled."

"Me, too."

"That rabbi bit was a beaut." Harry laughs a little in his throat. "He's good."

I look at Harry and smile. "He told me later that he wants to be an astronaut."

"Well, I guess he figured rabbi would impress me and astronaut would impress you. The kid's not stupid."

I don't reply.

"Mare?"

"Yeah?"

"Your mom and I have been talking, and we're wondering if we should report what Jacob did to the police. I mean, we really don't know what happened, how far he went, and . . . well . . . your mother thinks it's better that I talk to you. She thinks—"

"I know what she thinks." She thinks she wouldn't be the best person to question me about sex, but actually she would be.

"What do *you* think?" Harry asks.

I think maybe Jacob heard about Roxie's past and thought I'd be the same. Why else would he have chosen me? I'm such an idiot. "He didn't do anything to go to the police about."

Harry looks relieved. "Thank God." He sighs.

"I'm pretty sure he would have if we'd been somewhere else."

Harry doesn't say anything, just looks disgusted.

I take a small bite of muffin. "Abigail says it's my fault."

Harry's face changes to angry. "Your fault? Why?"

"Because we sat in the back row at the movies, and it was like saying it was okay for him to maul me."

Harry shakes his head. "I like Abigail, but she's dead wrong about that."

"She thinks you have to give in to guys or they'll find somebody who will."

Harry turns toward me, looks straight into my eyes. "Abigail doesn't know what she's talking about. All *that's* going to do is give a girl a bad reputation and make for some juicy talk in the boys' locker room." He hesitates. I suppose he's thinking about what happened to Roxie. "And make you a mother when you're still a kid."

"Like Roxie?"

He nods. "Just like Roxie."

"I know Roxie feels bad about getting pregnant in high school and the fact that everybody in town knows about Lonnie Kraft; but maybe she did me a favor, because I don't want the same thing to happen to me."

Harry smiles. "You're a smart girl, Mare. And you know what?"

"What?"

"It was the luckiest day in my life when you came into it."

I kiss Harry on the cheek. "It was the luckiest day in my life, too."

"Now how about you finish that English muffin, and we'll get you on the road."

! ! !

"That's perfect," Harry says after I parallel park for the first time ever. "You're a natural." I'm driving his everyday car: a '97 gray Ford Taurus, automatic.

"Thanks," I say. "Do you think we can go on the highway?"

"Don't see why not. You have city driving down pat."

I smile. "City?"

"You know what I mean," Harry says, fake exasperated.

I give him a yup-I-do look.

"Do you think you'd like to live in a city someday?" he asks as I pull out onto the street and head toward the interstate.

"I think so. I mean, I don't know for sure; but the times you've taken us to cities, I've liked them." I do know for sure. If I last that long without getting found out, I could get lost in the crowds of a city and maybe hide from my past forever. But I haven't heard from the guy in my head for a while, so maybe he's gone forever and it won't matter where I live.

"Slow down a little," Harry says as we turn onto Route 9 South—the road that leads to the interstate. "There's construction ahead."

The only thing I see in the distance is a guy on a bicycle coming toward us in the other lane. Suddenly, there's that same old pain in the back of my head, and I realize I was wrong. The voice is still around. *Hit the gas and plow that bastard down,* he says, playful. *It'll be fun, just like bowling.*

I try to shake the guy out of my head, but the pain gets so bad, I can hardly see. I speed up—almost in a trance—but as I'm veering to the left, toward the guy on the bike, Harry yells, "Maggie! You're going to hit that man!" And just like that, Harry's voice snaps me out of my daze, and I pull back into my lane. Then I step on the brake and slow down until the car comes to a complete stop on the side of the road.

"Good Lord, Mare," Harry says, frantic. "What happened?"

"I don't know!" I can't tell Harry what really went on. "I think I got the pedals mixed up, and then when I looked down, I went in the wrong lane." I focus on the rearview mirror, see the man still pedaling, and wonder if he has a wife and kids. He probably does—a mother, too, maybe. They all would have been devastated if I'd killed him. My heart starts pounding, and I'm fighting for every breath. Then the tears come, first one and then a river.

Harry holds me until I'm all washed out and then says, "That could have happened to anybody. No harm done." He pats his seat. "Slide over here, and I'll take us home."

As he's walking around to the driver's side, I realize that I won't need my learner's permit after all. A girl with a monster in her head has no business driving. I can feel my world shrinking. All I want to do is go home and stay there forever so nobody gets hurt.

I wish I could kill the man in my head, but to do that I would have to kill myself. I'm too much of a coward for that.

She's always been a little different.

D r. Scott is leaning back in the green leather chair, stifling a yawn.

I'm sitting at the end of the couch with my arms crossed, staring straight ahead.

Harry's next to me with his hands resting flat on his knees. He's wearing the Ralph Lauren cologne I got him last Christmas—a little too much.

Roxie's on the other side of Harry, perched at the edge of the couch, and her arms are flailing as she goes on about how she's at the end of her rope with me. "She sat around the house all summer, didn't go to the beach even once. And this girl's a regular fish, usually spends the entire summer in the water."

Dr. Scott looks at me. "Maggie, is there a reason why you didn't go to the beach this summer?"

I shrug. "I just didn't want to."

Roxie sighs. "See! That's what I've been dealing with. She doesn't want to do anything."

Again Dr. Scott looks at me. "Is that right, Maggie?"

"Yup," I say, blasé. "It's right."

"She's had her learner's permit for two months, and she won't even let us take her out driving. As soon as she gets her license, we're going to buy her a car as a belated birthday present—a brand-new black VW Beetle with a tan convertible top." Roxie looks at me, irritated. "She's been begging for one since last fall, and now she doesn't want it, says she won't drive it if we buy it."

Dr. Scott shifts in his chair a little with that one. "That sounds like a pretty sweet deal, Maggie. What's up with this?"

I'm thinking about the man I almost killed, and the thought must show in my eyes because Dr. Scott's are locked on them. "Do you want to talk about it?"

"No."

Harry looks over at me and says, "Is it okay if I do?"

I shrug again.

As Harry's telling Dr. Scott about my near miss, Roxie looks as if she's about to smack him if he doesn't let her talk. "That was just because she's a beginner," she finally says. "We've all had close calls when we were learning. Harry told me what happened. She just got the pedals mixed up." She stops to take a quick breath. "Why, a thing like that could happen to an experienced driver, too. Just before I bought my Mustang, my foot slipped off the brake onto the gas pedal, and I rammed my CR-V through the garage door and rear-ended the hearse—fifteen-thousand dollars worth of damage, including the door." She looks at the ceiling. "Thank God for insurance." She slaps her hands back and forth to signal *case closed* but adds, "That kind of thing happens to everybody."

Now we're all staring at Roxie as though *she* should be the one in therapy or at least under a microscope.

"So that really shook you up, did it?" Dr. Scott asks me.

I nod.

"Your mother's right, you know. We've all had scary things happen while we're driving."

With all due respect, Dr. Scott, normal scary things and having a jerk in your head who tells you to kill people aren't even close. "I know," I say. "I just don't want to drive right now. Maybe in a couple of years I'll try it again." I'll never try it again—ever!

"That makes sense." He looks at Roxie. "Don't you think so?"

"I guess," she says, not happy. "But it was going to be so much easier for me if I didn't have to drag her to all her after-school stuff."

"I'll ride my bike," I say. "Then you won't have to drive me anywhere." I am *so* back to not caring what people think about me. Riding my bike will be just fine. I don't think it's possible to kill somebody with a bicycle.

130

"You're going to ride your bike in the winter?" Roxie asks. "And in the rain?"

I give her the meanest look I can come up with. "I'll walk then. And take an umbrella."

"All right, we've got that solved," Dr. Scott says, fast. "Is there anything else you'd like to discuss, Mrs. Feigenbaum?" Dr. Scott looks at Harry with pity in his eyes. "Or you, Mr. Feigenbaum?"

Harry shakes his head. "No, I'm good."

Roxie must have saved the best for last, because right then she blurts out, "What about the time I found Mary-Magdalene sleeping in the casket room—in a casket, for God's sake?"

Oh, great. Just what I need. Dr. Scott sits up in his chair, Harry's straight-out hands turn into fists, and I slump down and try to disappear into the couch.

"She explained that to you," Harry says, angry. He looks at Dr. Scott. "She was afraid she'd wake us up with her nightmares, so she went downstairs to sleep. All the couches down there are covered in silk or some other expensive stuff, so she chose a display model." Harry laughs a little, but it's forced. "I've often wondered how comfortable they are." He looks at me and smiles. "I guess they're not too bad, because you slept right through the alarm on your phone."

"Weren't you scared?" Dr. Scott asks me. There's shock in his voice.

"No. Not at all," I say nonchalantly. "One of my jobs since I was a little girl has been to clean the casket room. They're just

131

like beds, only fancier." It's true that I wasn't scared, and it's true that I didn't want to wake up Harry and Roxie with my nightmares. Plus, now that Roxie opened her big, fat mouth, Dr. Scott knows for sure that I'm as crazy as a loon. But having him think of me as a morbid weirdo is oh so much better than him knowing what I really am.

"*I* would have been scared," Dr. Scott says. I don't know if he's telling the truth or just trying to get me to say more.

Since this has nothing to do with the voice in my head, I do. "I also wanted to find out what being dead and laid out feels like," I say as if I'm discussing the weather. "It's not too bad. The casket itself is kind of hard, but the pillow is nice."

Dr. Scott stares at me as if he just found out that I drink blood.

"Haven't you ever wondered what it would be like to be dead?" I ask.

Roxie starts to say something, but Dr. Scott cuts her off. "Do you think about death a lot, Maggie?" That's what he always does. If I ask him a personal question, he pretends he didn't hear it and keeps hammering away at me. I guess that's what shrinks are trained to do.

"Well, I live in a house where there's usually at least one dead person lying around, so I probably think about it more than most kids."

Roxie can't stand it another minute and blurts out, "She's always been a little different, but there's nothing wrong with that."

"Different, how?" Dr. Scott asks.

"I don't know. Like when she was little and talked to that imaginary friend of hers." She looks at me. "What was her name?"

Oh, God. Please kill me now. "Penelope."

"Right, Penelope," Roxie says. "Mary-Magdalene used to have long conversations with a kid that wasn't even there." She gives Dr. Scott a worried look. "But that's normal, though, right?"

Dr. Scott nods. "Very normal, especially with only children."

"So there you go," Roxie concludes. "She just has an overactive imagination."

Harry looks at Roxie, confused, as if he's trying to figure out what having an imaginary friend and sleeping in a casket have in common.

Dr. Scott skips over Roxie and returns to me since I am the main loon. "Well, Maggie, now that you know what sleeping in a casket feels like, are you going to continue?"

I know what he wants me to say, so I do. "No. I'm done with that. But I still don't see what the big deal is."

Harry puts his arm around my shoulder. "It's not a big deal, Mare. It's just that unless you live in an environment like we do, things like that seem a lot creepier than they really are."

"Your dad's right," Dr. Scott says, not very convincingly. "It's not a big deal, but I wouldn't recommend it." He smiles. "I'm sure your bed's a lot more comfortable."

I smile back. "Right," I say.

He looks at the clock, which shows that we're way over our time, but this must be more entertaining for him than watching a horror movie. "Well, we'll stop there," he says as if he's dealing with sane people. He looks straight at Roxie. "I want to thank you for coming, Mrs. Feigenbaum. I'm sure your input will move things along." When he looks at Harry, Dr. Scott sighs. I bet he's wondering how Harry got mixed up with Roxie and me. "And thank you, Mr. Feigenbaum. You've been a big help, too."

"Do we have to come to the next appointment?" Roxie asks. "I had to change my salon time, and they're not very flexible about—"

"No, no, that's fine," Dr. Scott replies. "Today's visit will give Maggie and me plenty of things to talk about for quite a while."

Dr. Scott shakes Harry's hand and pats him on the shoulder the way people do when they're offering sympathy.

On our way out the door, Dr. Scott pats me on the shoulder, too. "See you in a week, Maggie," he says, all cheery. But his eyes are full of concern, and I have a feeling that it won't be long before he figures out what I really am.

How pregnant are you?

I never thought I'd say this, but I'm glad that school has finally started. Since I was just sitting around the house, Roxie put me to work scrubbing it. I now know everything there is to know about disinfecting bathrooms, scouring refrigerators, and polishing hardwood floors. If the veterinarian thing doesn't work out, I'll be qualified to open a full-service cleaning business.

It's lunchtime, and I'm sitting in the cafeteria at the table in the corner with the chipped trays and extra silverware. I'm in a rotten mood because I woke up with my period and the cramps are so bad, I feel like smacking God. I guess giving girls a bloody mess every month wasn't bad enough, so he threw in fall-over-dead pains to boot. My back is to the other kids, and I'm reading *Anna Karenina*, the part where she throws herself under the train. This is so disturbing that I close the book, cross my arms on the table, and rest my head on them.

"Maggie?" Abigail's voice startles me and I sit up fast.

"Hi," I say friendly-like, before I remember that I'm mad at her. Little by little, Allison Jamison and her stuck-up cronies wrapped Abigail in their cocoon, and until now, she only said hi when she saw me in the hall.

"Is it okay if I sit down?" Her tone is timid, and she's standing back as though she's contaminated.

"Sure, go ahead." I've been so lonely and I've really missed her, but I can't read her face. This could go either way, but just having her here feels good. It's like after you've been on a long trip: when you get home, it's so nice to be back and to sleep in your own bed again.

She sits across from me, doesn't say anything. Just stares at her lap.

I don't know *what* to say, so we're more like strangers on a bus than used-to-be best friends. When I glance over at her, I notice that her pretty new look is still there, but it seems to have gone a little dull. I don't think she washed her hair this morning, and her pastel face is pale, no pink at all. "Abigail?" I say, low.

She looks up. "Yeah?"

"What's the matter?"

"Nothing," she says, too fast to be convincing. Then she adds, "I just don't feel very well."

I rub my belly. "I don't either. I got my period, and I feel like crap."

She peers down at her lap again. "I wish I'd gotten mine."

"You do? Why?"

She looks over at me with desperation in her eyes.

Oh.

"You were right about Jacob. I should have listened to you."

"Damn! What happened?" Well, that was stupid. "I mean, I know what happened, but . . . what *happened*?"

"I did everything the magazines said to do, set boundaries and let him know how far I'd go."

Oh, brother. I feel sorry for her because she actually believes that the stuff in those magazines works.

"At first he was a perfect gentleman, and I thought he wasn't attracted to me—I mean in *that* way." She looks down at her flat front, then over at my way-too-curvy one. "I thought maybe he only liked girls with . . ."

I help her out. "Big badoinkees?"

She giggles like the old Abigail.

"I think that's the only reason he asked me out," I say, candid.

The giggles disappear, and Abigail continues her story. "But then he made his move." She gets a faraway look in her eye and adds, "Did you know he used to be a wrestler in his old school? He was on the varsity team in his freshman year."

"I didn't know that." But it explains how a guy who's not much taller than I am and just as skinny can force a girl to do anything he wants her to. I think how neither Abigail nor I are anywhere near ready for the real world. But then I remember that it's too late for Abigail to wait until she *is* ready.

"He's so strong. I couldn't get him off," she says.

I look over at the tray of extra silverware; most of it beat-up and bent from the stupid boys showing off. *Watch what I can do to this itsy-bitsy fork.* Jerks! "I know," I say. "I was just lucky."

But then her story makes a sudden U-turn. "When he really got into it, I liked it. It felt good. I didn't want him to stop."

I'm so shocked, I simply stare at her, say nothing.

"After that we started using condoms, but it was too late."

The dam in Abigail's heart must have broken, because a flood of tears flows down her face and she just keeps sitting there.

I should know what to do. This is like the dream I have where it's time for the final test, and I haven't even been to one class yet. I reach in my lunch bag, hand her the scrunched-up napkin with the mustard stains from my ham and cheese sandwich. She grabs it as though it's made of silk.

"Thanks," she says after she cleans up the mess of snot and tears.

"Does your mother know?" I think of Mrs. Flute and her I'm-better-than-you attitude.

"No!" Abigail looks panic stricken. "She can't ever know. My father either."

"But . . ."

She grabs my arm, looks at me as if I might betray her

because of the way she's been treating me. "You won't tell them, will you?"

"Of course not. I was just wondering if you had."

Her body relaxes. "All I want to do is forget about what happened and go on with my life."

I think about that night in the movies. "I know how you feel." But her situation is so much worse. "Well, I don't *really* know how you feel. I just . . . I just . . . I don't know what to say."

"I need your help," Abigail says, desperate.

"But what can I do?"

"I have to get rid of it."

I know Abigail has no idea what I really am, so why do I think she's treating me like a hit man?

I picture a tiny version of Ali Rogers nestled all safe inside Abigail, dressed in one of those onesie outfits decorated with rosebuds. Abigail is so feminine looking that I can't imagine her having anything but a girl. Maybe she could call her Amy, which sounds as soft as a baby. But then I remember the embryo chart the health teacher showed us in middle school: little bug-eyed pollywogs are how they start out.

"How big is it?" I ask.

"What?"

"I mean, how pregnant are you?"

"I don't know. A few weeks, I guess. I'm a month overdue for my period."

"Well, maybe you're just late. Sometimes I—"

"I'm not late. I took one of those pregnancy tests, and it turned bright blue."

*Well, then it's a boy* is what comes into my head. I am such a dunce. "Oh," I say. "From what I hear, those things are pretty accurate."

"I have an appointment on Wednesday to . . . well, you know." She gives me a pleading look. "Will you come with me? The woman I talked to on the phone said that because it's so early, it should be pretty easy."

"Doesn't your mother have to take you? Won't she have to sign something?"

"No. Not in New York State. I could go alone, but I'd really like you to come for moral support."

I think how you can't even go on a field trip unless one of your parents gives written permission, but you can do this adult thing on your own.

"Well, will you?" Her eyes are saying *please*.

"I'll come," I say. I don't want to, and until now I didn't even know how I felt about abortion. You'd think a girl who has killed two fully formed people wouldn't care about ending the life of a pollywog. But I do.

ˈ ˈ ˈ

When Wednesday afternoon comes, I sit in the waiting room at Planned Parenthood while Abigail is in one of the closed-door rooms in the back. I try to concentrate on the magazine I'm holding: *Bon Appétit*. So far I have learned that I can cut calories if I substitute applesauce for sour cream in my banana bread. I think how smart that is until I remember that I hate banana bread, banana anything, for that matter. I close the magazine, toss it back on the coffee table in front of me, and wonder how Abigail's doing.

I'm looking at a poster on the wall that shows a sad-looking girl cradling her huge belly when I hear a door open behind me and then Abigail's voice. "I'm done," she says, low. She's standing next to me, and she looks regular, except her hair's a little disheveled.

"You're all right?" I ask. I don't know what I expected, but something a lot more dramatic than this.

"Yeah, I'm okay. Let's just go."

"Can you walk home or do you want me to call Harry? We can wait up the street on the bench near the post office. We don't even have to tell him where we've been."

"I can walk."

When we get outside, I say, "Did it hurt?"

She shakes her head and smiles. "I wasn't even pregnant, just late. Can you believe it? I was worried about nothing."

"But what about the pregnancy test? I thought those things were pretty accurate."

"I did, too, but the nurse said that I must have waited too long to read it. I guess you have to follow the directions exactly."

Well, *yeah*. I think it would be a good idea. "I didn't know that either," I say so she doesn't feel too dumb.

Then she adds, "I remember my mother called me to ask

about something while I was waiting; and when I went back, the test looked positive."

Neither of us says a word all the way home. She's probably still trying to process what just happened. When we get to her house, I expect her to ask me to come in, but she doesn't. Instead, she says, "Thanks again, Maggie. I couldn't have done this without you."

"That's okay." She probably didn't sleep a wink last night. Maybe she's going to go lie down and she'll call me tomorrow.

"Well, bye then," she says on her way up the front steps. "I have to let Jacob know that everything's just fine."

As I watch her go inside, I realize that I won't hear from her again unless she has another emergency. I think of the word *loyal* in the dictionary. This time Abigail's picture does not come to mind.

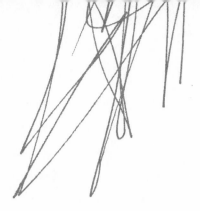

Maybe this is what it feels like to be dead.

r. Scott's wearing khaki pants and a short-sleeved polo shirt—not Ralph Lauren Polo, the generic kind with no insignia sewn on the front. I like this because it shows he's confident enough about himself that he doesn't need Ralph Lauren's or some other famous designer's help to prove that he's with-it. Since Jacob turned out to be a dud, I have gone back to fantasizing about Dr. Scott and me.

"I've been thinking about meeting my birth father," I blurt out fast before I lose my nerve or change my mind.

"Really?" He stops at that. Maybe it's not such a good idea after all.

143

"Yup." The bulb in the lamp beside him flickers. He reaches over to tighten it—a chance to slow my breathing.

"You've never mentioned your birth father."

"Well, I kind of thought I didn't have to. Everybody in town knows about him." I wonder if Dr. Scott will pretend that he's never heard about Lonnie Kraft just to make me feel better.

He nods. "I guess that's true."

I thought so. "Yeah."

"What do you think you'll gain by meeting him?" he asks in his professional voice.

I want to know what he sounds like, that's all. "I don't know. Just what he's like, I guess."

"Do you want to know if he thinks about you?"

No. I don't care one tiny bit about that. "Yes. I wonder about that all the time."

"That's natural, especially for a girl your age."

"That what I've heard." Sometimes I scare myself because I'm such a good liar.

"Have you talked to your parents about this?"

I nod. "I spoke with Harry, and he's going to talk to my mother."

"You seem to have a much more open relationship with your stepfather than you do with your mother." Dr. Scott's voice is make-you-faint sexy: not too high, not too low, just perfect.

"I do," I answer, trying to concentrate on the conversation instead of him.

"Why do you think that is?"

I don't respond right away because I've never thought about it. "Harry doesn't judge me," I say finally. "He just loves me the way I am."

"I'm sure your mother loves you, too," Dr. Scott says. "It's often harder for mothers and daughters to get along."

You can say that again. "Yeah, I suppose, but sometimes she can be pretty critical."

"Maggie, it's difficult for some people to express their emotions. Sometimes they kick and snarl at the ones they love the most because it's more comfortable than showing how they really feel. Especially if that's the way they were raised. It's what they're used to—all they know."

Oh, a bad nip at my heart. "My mother never told me anything about her parents, only that they were dead because of a car accident."

"Well, from what she's told me on the phone, they weren't exactly what you'd call loving, especially her father."

"What did he do?" I've never met him, and I hate him already.

"She didn't say. You'll have to ask her about it."

It never occurred to me that Roxie might have been treated badly when she was growing up. When we have our little tiffs, the only person I think about is me. Sometimes you have to take a step back and examine yourself. And sometimes what you see makes you feel like dirt.

! ! !

I'm riding my bike home from Dr. Scott's, taking the shortcut down by the river, when I see Patty-Ann Thurston sitting on the side of the road next to her tricycle that's smashed to smithereens. Tears are streaming down her face, and she's whimpering like a little girl.

I get off my bike, kneel next to her, and put my hand on her shoulder. At first she pulls away, but when she sees who I am, she puts her arms around my neck and hangs on like a vise.

Finally, she calms down and loosens her grip. "What happened, Patty-Ann?" I say, gentle, like you'd talk to a child.

"I'd just started off toward town to the American Legion Hall for the big harvest supper they put on every year." She reaches into her pocket and brings out a light-blue ticket. "They gave me this free over at the senior center." I guess she forgot she was in the middle of a story because she just clams up.

"Then what happened?"

"It was that mean Joe Matte. He was following behind me in his truck, kept honking his horn for me to get out of the way. I moved over as much as I could, but he still kept honking even though he could have gone around; there's hardly ever a car passes by here. Then he pulled over, got out, shoved me onto the road, and beat up my bike with a baseball bat. Said if I told anybody, he'd burn down my trailer." She looks at me with desperation in her eyes and gestures toward the rusty single-wide on a hill behind her. "If he does that, I won't have anything, no place to sleep even."

Joe Matte's the town bully. He's been arrested on assault

charges for as long as I can remember. They ought to lock him up for good and save some wear and tear on the jail door. "Did he do anything to you, Patty-Ann?" I ask. "I mean, did he hurt you?"

She shakes her head. "Just called me a stupid retard like he always does." She tries to put a broken spoke in the wheel of her bike, but it falls back out.

The pain has started up in the back of my head. I want to ignore it, but I can't. It's as if I'm being stabbed with a knife. "Where is he now?" I whisper, barely able to speak.

She points to the bridge in the distance. "He's over there fishing. You can see his truck if you look real good."

"I can see him," I say. I stand then help her up. "Come on. Let's get you home."

"What about my bike?" Patty-Ann worries.

"The wheels are broken, and it's too heavy to carry. I guess you'll just have to leave it here."

"I'd like to kill that man," Patty-Ann says. She reaches for my hand as we head toward her house. "I hope he falls into the river and drowns."

"Will you be able to get to the supper without your bike?" I ask. I'm sure Harry would come and give her a ride.

"Oh, I'll get there, all right." She points at her feet. "I'm not too proud to hoof it. Those American Legion people make the best apple pie in the world, better than my mama used to make." She scowls at the layers of clothes she's wearing. "I just need to clean myself up a little."

As I'm walking toward my bike, the pain lessens but then the voice comes. *See that rock on the side of the road? The big one?*

I nod.

*Put it in your tote bag.*

"It won't fit."

*Make it fit!*

I unzip my denim tote bag with the dark-green trim and take out the library books I was planning to return. Then I shove the rock in the bag, force the zipper shut, and put everything in my bicycle basket.

*You know what you have to do,* the voice says low and slow and deliberate.

I look over at Joe Matte and think of how he's tormented Patty-Ann for so long. Then I get on my bike and pedal toward him. When I get close, I stop and lean my bike against the railing on the opposite side of the bridge. He has on headphones, and I can hear strains of heavy metal blaring. I don't even think he knows I'm here. But just in case, I pretend I need something from my tote bag, take it out of the basket, and inch in his direction. He must have seen me riding toward him, because he turns to face me, lowers the volume of the music, takes off the headphones, and wears them like a necklace. I walk over, stand next to him, put my tote bag down, and lean my arms on the railing.

*What are you doing?* the voice asks, impatient. *You could have clobbered him by now.*

The pain in my head is starting up again. "I know what to do," I say under my breath.

"Catch anything?" I ask Joe Matte. He's a big man, tall and stocky. He's wearing jeans and a short-sleeved shirt, clean.

"Who the hell are you?" He glares at me as if I've come to steal his fish.

"Maggie Feigenbaum." I point to the books in my bike basket. "I'm on my way to the library."

*Why are you making small talk? Get on with it!*

I look away from Joe, whisper to the voice, "Wait a minute!"

"Oh, yeah," Joe Matte says. "You're the mortician's kid."

"Right." The thought of Harry jolts me back to Earth—like in the car. Maybe I don't have to kill Joe. Maybe I can just talk him out of hurting Patty-Ann.

*"Well?"* Joe says, not mean, just totally dumbfounded.

"Well what?"

"What do you want?"

*Good grief, Maggie. You're killing me here.*

"I was just wondering why you ruined Patty-Ann's bike?"

Now Joe gets mean. "What's it to you?"

"I was wondering what she did that made you so mad." I look down toward the river as if I'm interested in the rocks. "I mean, I know she can be frustrating and I figured she must have done something pretty bad to make you angry enough to smash her bike like that."

*This guy's a felon, Maggie. You know that. He doesn't deserve to live after what he did to Patty-Ann. Think of poor Patty-Ann.*

"You're goddamned right she can be frustrating," Joe continues. "They oughtn't to let her live among regular people.

They should put her in one of those homes for folks who aren't right in the head. She'd be happier with other retards who don't expect her to act normal."

*He's totally heartless. Can't you see that?*

My insides knot up, and I think how Patty-Ann would die in a place like that. I feel the headache starting again, but I take a long, deep breath and try to shake it off. "So what did she do, get in your way?"

"Get in my way? Hells bells. She was riding that stupid bike of hers right down the middle of the road, swerving back and forth like a fool in a fit—singing one of those songs from a TV show for kids."

I fake a laugh. "Sounds like something Patty-Ann would do."

*So now you two are pals?*

Joe looks at me and frowns. "You wouldn't think it was so funny if you were trying to get by her and she was acting like she owned the road."

I look at him and shake my head. "No, I guess I wouldn't."

"I kept trying to get around her, but because of the way she was riding, I almost hit her. Finally, I couldn't stand it anymore, so I got out of my truck and told her to get off the thing. Then I took my baseball bat to it. It's what any normal guy would have done." He sighs huge, as if he's reliving the whole thing. "It was better than killing her like I wanted to do."

I nod. "You're right. It was." This man is so much better than I am.

*Come on, Maggie. The men you killed deserved it. Quit feeling sorry for yourself. Finish this one off and let's go.*

"Besides, she shouldn't be allowed to ride that thing in the road," Joe continues. "She's gonna cause a bad accident some-day, so I did everybody a favor."

*Look how he's making excuses. Clock him!*

"She said you threatened to burn down her trailer if she told anybody." I look him straight in the eye. "You were kidding, right?"

He reels in his line a little, sees the empty hook, and frowns. "Yeah. Sure. Okay. I was kidding." He looks at me, suspicious. "Why are you so interested in Patty-Ann Thurston? What's she to you?"

I shrug. "Just a friend of the family."

*Ah, jeez, Maggie. You're hopeless.*

Joe laughs in his throat. "You sure got some mixed-up family there. An old geezer for a father and a sweet-lookin' chick for a mother. How'd that fat old Jew latch onto such a foxy little lady?" He stares off into space. "I sure would like a chance at her."

Rage boils inside of me, and the pain in my head is back worse than ever. It's as if a hundred sledgehammers are pound-ing on my skull.

*You can't let that ignorant bastard diss Harry and Roxie like that. Kill him!*

As I pick up my tote bag, Joe Matte grabs my arm and ogles me up and down. "You know. You're not that bad yourself.

Looks like you inherited your mom's sexy bod." He laughs a little then narrows his eyes. "I bet you aren't here about Patty-Ann at all. I think what you want is a little action."

I try to pull my arm out of his grasp, but he tightens it. Then he looks around, checking to see if we're alone. I guess we are, because he says, "I bet you've never been with a man before. Probably just kissed a few of those pimply faced teenagers. And you know what they say: like mother, like daughter." He tries to force me to the ground; but he's still holding his fishing pole with his other hand, so he loses his grip on me.

I back away from him and hold my tote bag with both hands. As he comes toward me, I swing the bag like a club—so hard that the strap breaks. As the rock inside connects with Joe Matte's head, he falls to the ground, no blood at all.

I open the tote, throw the rock over the railing, and head for my bike. Before I start pedaling, I look back and see Patty-Ann watching me from the road at the end of the bridge. She's just standing there with her arms hanging straight down like a marionette, with a strange look on her face as if she can't believe what she just saw.

The only thing that comes to mind is that Lester is going to win after all. And when he does, Harry's heart will break wide-open.

After I return my books, I ride around to the back of the library and throw my tote bag into the Dumpster. It's no good with a broken strap. But more important, there's dirt inside from the crime scene and probably Joe Matte's hair and DNA on the outside. When Patty-Ann tells the police what she saw, Lester will come forward about his father and Mr. Sullivan, and nobody will believe that Joe Matte's death was self-defense. The police will search everything I own to find evidence that will prove that I murdered him.

I wonder what prison will be like. Cold, I bet.

ɪ ɪ ɪ

"How was your session with Dr. Scott?" Roxie asks when I get to the kitchen.

"It was okay, but I have a lot of homework. Is it all right if we talk later?"

Her face drops. "Sure, I guess so."

If I don't leave right this minute, I'm going to keel over.

When I get to my room, I lie on my bed and stare at the ceiling. The inside of my head has gone black. Then I shiver as if all the blood in my body has suddenly turned to ice. Maybe this is what it feels like to be dead.

## Stupid like a Fox.

"It's time to get up," Roxie says. "You've been asleep since you got home yesterday. I couldn't even wake you for dinner." She's sitting on the side of my bed. Her legs are crossed, and the top one is bouncing bad. "Are you feeling okay?"

I forget for a second, and then the memory of the bridge and what I did slams into me so hard I can barely take a breath. I think of the tote bag in the Dumpster. Why'd I leave it there in plain sight? I should have buried it. I have to get it back! I look over at Roxie and think how she *so* doesn't deserve what's coming.

"I'm fine," I say, trying to sound convincing. "My therapy sessions always wear me out."

"Well, you get ready, and I'll make you some breakfast. Eggs or cereal?"

"Cereal's fine, but I can get it." I couldn't eat one bite, but this way she won't know and ask me a million questions that I would have to make up lies for.

"Okay then, I'll go get myself cleaned up."

She's nearly out of my room when she turns and adds, "Something terrible happened yesterday afternoon—probably when you were at Dr. Scott's."

A hard blow to the stomach. "Really? What?" I picture a policeman at our door, Harry crying. Roxie, too, maybe.

"Joe Matte was found dead, and they've taken in Patty-Ann Thurston for questioning, so I guess they must think she killed him. At least that's what they reported on last night's eleven-o'clock news."

What Roxie said is so wrong, it doesn't register at first. "Patty-Ann didn't kill anybody," I say.

Roxie looks at me funny.

"I mean, she's so old. And I've never heard anything about her being violent."

"Well, it does seem strange," Roxie agrees, "but that's what it said on the news. I haven't read this morning's paper yet."

As soon as I hear Roxie's bathroom door close, I race to the kitchen. The newspaper is on the counter. The lead story on the front page: "Area Man Found Murdered on Ausable River Bridge, Local Woman Questioned." I do my best to read the article, but my hands are shaking so much I can hardly see the words.

▾ ▾ ▾

I'm barely out the door when Lester Pint appears and starts walking to school with me. This is the first time he's come anywhere near me since that day at his pool.

"Hey, Maggie," he says, confident, as if he's finally got me trapped under his paw. "Did you read today's paper?"

"No." I pick up the pace. He matches it.

"You didn't?" His tone says he doesn't believe me.

"I hardly ever read the paper."

"Well, you should have read today's."

I give him a get-lost look.

"There's been another murder."

"Oh, yeah?"

"Joe Matte was bludgeoned to death on the Ausable River Bridge."

Inside I'm quivering, but on the surface I stay calm. "And why should this interest me?"

"The paper said the police questioned Patty-Ann Thurston because they found that crazy-looking tricycle of hers all bashed in on the road by her house. A baseball bat in Joe Matte's truck had matching blue paint all over it. And the article said that his

156

skull was crushed by a blunt object, probably a rock." He's not telling me anything I don't already know, but hearing it makes it seem even worse.

"What does this have to do with me?" I ask, all snotty-like. Although I feel like falling over, I keep walking, don't give him the satisfaction of looking at him.

"The article said that Patty-Ann's doctor said she couldn't possibly have committed the crime because she's so short and too weak."

"Sounds right," I say. "Plus, Patty-Ann wouldn't hurt anybody."

"But she told them who did it and then they let her go."

Bile rises in my throat. "Good," I say, and I mean it. "I'm glad they let her go. She doesn't belong in jail."

Lester picks up the pace, turns around, walks backward, and stares me straight in the eye. "Are you really glad?" he asks with a sneer in his voice. "We both know it doesn't bother you to hurt people."

"Lester, get away from me." I try to go by him, but he does that little back-and-forth dance thing, so I can't.

"All right, I'll go," he says, "but this time you're going to get what's coming to you."

He takes off running in his nerdy way, and I slow down. Lester's right. This time I *am* going to get what's coming to me. The police will probably show up at school and arrest me right in front of everybody. Then Lester can tell them about his father and Mr. Sullivan, and it won't matter that he doesn't have any proof. If I could murder Joe Matte, it makes sense that I could kill those other two men.

I take a detour toward the library. When I pass the Dumpster, I see that my tote bag is gone. It's probably with some forensic scientist who's testing it for DNA and fibers right this very minute. Now that Patty-Ann has told the police that I killed Joe Matte, they'll have all the evidence they need.

𝁜 𝁜 𝁜

I'm in the living room watching the six-o'clock news. A reporter is standing next to Patty-Ann in front of her trailer, interviewing her.

"Can you describe the man who stopped to help you?"

"He was big."

"Big how? Do you mean tall or hefty?"

"Both. Kind of like that Incredible Hulk guy, only not green."

The reporter looks as though he's trying to stifle a smile. "What about his hair color?"

"There was no color."

"So it was white?"

"Isn't white a color?"

"I don't know," the reporter says. "Maybe not. Can you describe his hair?"

"No."

"So he was wearing a hat."

"No."

"Then what was his hair like?"

"He didn't have any. That man was as bald as a turnip."

The reporter does not look amused, but he goes back for more. "What about his eye color?"

"What about it?" Patty-Ann says.

"Do you remember what color his eyes were?"

"No."

"Try to think back to when he was right next to you."

"It won't do any good. I could stand here and think all day, and I still wouldn't be able to tell you what color eyes he had."

"Why's that?"

"He was wearing sunglasses—the wraparound kind they give you after you have your cataracts cut off."

"So he was an older man."

"No, he was kind of young."

"But you just said . . ." The reporter doesn't say "Oh, never mind," but that must be what he's thinking. He gives up on the description and takes a different path.

"After this person stopped in the road to see if you were all right, what happened next?"

"He asked me where Joe Matte went after he beat up my bike. I pointed to where Joe was fishing over on the bridge."

"And then what happened?"

"The man who stopped to help me picked up a big rock from the side of the road and got back in his car."

"Did you see where he went?"

"Sure I did. I have eyes, don't I? Over to Joe Matte on the bridge."

"Could you see what the man did then?"

"Course I could see. I followed him. Saw everything clear as I can see you right now."

"And what did you see?"

"That man walked over to Joe Matte and slammed that rock smack hard into the side of Joe's head. Joe fell down. The man threw the rock in the river, went back to his car, and took off. That's all I know." Patty-Ann turns around and heads toward the steps of her trailer.

"Didn't Joe Matte try to defend himself?"

Patty-Ann shrugs. "Didn't seem to. If he did, I missed that part." She takes a wad of gum out of her mouth, holds it up so the reporter can get a good look. "Maybe when I was getting the pack of Juicy Fruit out of my pocket."

Patty-Ann returns the gum to her mouth and opens the door of her trailer. "I have to go. I got soup on the stove—vegetable beef—the chunky kind with noodles."

"Just one more question," the reporter says.

"Okay, but can you make it quick?"

"Have you ever seen the man before?"

"Who? Joe Matte? Sure, I've seen him lots of times. He made fun of me for as long as I can remember. I'm glad he's dead. I hope he's burning in you-know-where."

"No, Miss Thurston, I mean the man who stopped to help you."

"Oh, him. No, I never saw him before in my life. I don't think he was from around here. He had a funny license plate."

The reporter's voice ramps up. "Funny how?"

"Well, for one, it was the wrong color—red or blue or green, maybe. And it had more numbers than the ones around here with letters mixed in. And he didn't talk like regular people."

"How *did* he talk?"

"I don't know. Just kind of funny, like he might have been a cowboy or from one of those down-low states. Florida maybe, or California."

The reporter's face looks pained. "Can you describe the car?"

"I already did for the police. I told them all this stuff."

"Will you tell *us* what it looked like?"

"It was regular: doors, windows, you know."

"What about the color?"

"Brown, I think. Or blue maybe. Could have even been black or gray. Not red, though. I would have remembered red. It's my favorite color. Look, I have to go. I bet my soup's boiled all over my stove by now. Probably nothing left of it." Before Patty-Ann disappears into her trailer, she looks straight into the camera and says, "If the person who got rid of Joe Matte is watching this, I just want to say thanks." And then she's gone.

The reporter looks stunned as he says, "Rob Bruner, Channel Five News. Back to you, Steve."

Steve thanks Rob for his report and then announces that there will be donation boxes in all the local businesses to collect money to replace Patricia-Ann Thurston's three-wheeler. Steve

161

hopes everyone will be extra generous because of everything Ms. Thurston has been through.

After Patty-Ann's piece, my body unwinds, and I can take a full breath for the first time since this whole thing began. I go to my room to get started on my homework. I can imagine how the viewing audience must be laughing their heads off because they think Patty-Ann sounded so stupid. *Stupid like a fox* is what I think.

I'm you. The real you.

"Are you sure you want to do this?" Roxie asks. We're on our way to the Clinton Correctional Facility in Dannemora. Even though she's going to wait in another room while I talk to Lonnie Kraft, she's as tense as I am, white-knuckling the steering wheel, which she never does; she usually drives one-handed, the big-deal way. It's cold today, so she has the top up on the Mustang. Most of the trees are bare, and a lot of the houses we're passing are decorated for Halloween.

"I'm sure," I say." Then to make it even more definite, I add, "Dr. Scott thinks it's a good idea."

"Well, I guess I knew this day would come," she says with a sigh. "I just wasn't looking forward to it."

"Roxie?" I ask. "Did you ever come to visit him?"

"Never," she says. "I couldn't see the point. We'd broken up before he . . . well, you know the story."

"Does he even know about me?"

"He knew there was going to be a baby, but that's all." Then with relief in her voice because I'll stop asking questions about Lonnie Kraft, she says, "Here's Dannemora. I guess you'll find out soon enough."

The only thing I see is an enormous cement wall with guard towers that goes on for miles. It's as though the whole town is a prison. You can see men in the towers ready to shoot prisoners who try to escape, although I can't imagine anybody even thinking about getting over *that* wall. As Roxie turns into a driveway with a sign that reads VISITOR ENTRANCE, my stomach contracts, and I think this might not be such a good idea after all.

꜡ ꜡ ꜡

I'm sitting at the end of a bolted-to-the-floor metal table in an otherwise empty room by myself when the door opens. A corrections officer follows a tall, skinny man in a dark-green uniform who's wearing handcuffs and has a chain connecting his ankles that makes him take quick little baby steps. He has a regular combed-over haircut with a part on the side and his skin is vampire white and sprinkled with rust-colored freckles, no skull-and-crossbones tattoo like I thought there might be. When he sits down at the opposite end of the table, he looks straight at

164

me. His eyes are the same shape and light blue as mine, only *his* look worn-out, no spark at all.

The corrections officer locks Lonnie Kraft's handcuffs to a contraption on the end of the table, then stands directly behind him, which makes me feel safe. But I'm thinking about the questions I want to ask, and I wonder if what we say has to be kept a secret like at the doctor's office. The corrections officer looks more like he's wondering what his wife will serve for dinner than what Lonnie Kraft and I are about to say, so I stop worrying about that.

I'm trying to figure out how to start when Lonnie Kraft jumps right in. "So you're Roxie's girl."

That answers my first question. His voice doesn't sound anything like the one in my head. "Yes. I'm Maggie."

"You're real pretty, Maggie, just like your mother," he says. I can tell he means it, but doesn't he see that I look like him?

"Thanks," I say. I like that he's not taking any credit for me and that he thought Roxie was pretty.

"How is she?" he asks in a gentle tone.

"Fine. She's fine."

He rests his wrists on the edge of the table and does that here's-the-church-here's-the-steeple thing with his fingers. "The man she married—is he good to her?"

"Really good."

"I'm glad. She deserves to be happy."

He lets out a half laugh, the kind where one side of your

mouth stays put and the other side goes up a little. "She was one of the shyest girls I've ever known."

"Roxie was shy?" How can that be?

"Maybe more quiet than shy, but I think that's because her father was so strict." He looks troubled. "Is he still alive?"

"No. He and my grandmother were killed in a car crash before I was born."

"Well, I'm sorry about your grandmother."

"Thanks," I reply, even though I have no feelings about either of them. But what Lonnie Kraft just said makes me wonder why he isn't sorry about Roxie's father. Then I remember what Dr. Scott said about her father not being loving, and it makes me feel bad all over again.

"That's strange about Roxie being shy," I say. "I heard that she was pretty popular in high school. That she was . . . well . . ."

He looks confused. "Do you mean easy?"

"That's what I heard." I hope he doesn't ask me who said it. Telling him it was a man in my head would be a little awkward.

"Whoever told you that doesn't know what they're talking about. I was her only boyfriend; and when her father found out that she was pregnant, he made her break up with me . . . and then this other mess happened."

The corrections officer is checking his watch, so I think I'd better get a move on. "I was wondering if you could tell me about my relatives on your side—you know, for medical reasons." Especially the insane ones.

"Sure, but I come from pretty healthy stock." He shifts in

his seat. "Except my mother." Oh, right. The one he beat to death.

"What was wrong with her?" I ask, expecting him to say heart trouble or cancer or something like that.

"Nothing physically."

"Well then, what?"

"She heard voices." The shock of what he just said is keeping me locked to this chair as tightly as the chains that are holding him.

"Voices? You mean like imaginary ones in her head?"

"She said that a man's voice came to her and told her to do evil things."

"What kinds of evil things?"

I wonder if he's noticed how my voice is cracking. But he's just sitting there, biting his bottom lip.

Finally he says, "Like murdering people."

My stomach tightens. "Did she do what he told her to? I mean, did she ever kill anybody?"

"If she did, she was never caught."

"What did her doctors say about it? I mean, why wasn't she in a hospital or something?"

"Nobody knew about it but me. And I thought she was making it up. She was always so gentle."

"What did your mother sound like?" I ask. "I mean, what was her voice like?" She has to be the person in my head. Maybe she was a heavy smoker. Sometimes women who smoke sound like men.

"She had a sweet voice. You'd never know she had an evil side."

"Huh" is all I say. It's hard to process so much stuff. "Do you mind if I ask you one more question, even though you probably won't want to answer it?"

"That's all right. Ask away."

"Why did you kill your mother?"

He doesn't even hesitate like I thought he would. "She was coming at me with a butcher knife. It was out of the blue. One minute we were discussing what we were having for supper and the next she was talking to somebody who wasn't there and trying to kill me. I pushed her away, and she hit her head on the corner of the counter." His shoulders droop. "Not many jurors believe a mother who'd never been arrested in her life would try to kill her own son because a voice in her head told her to."

"But rumor has it that you killed her with a meat pounder because she cooked your eggs wrong."

He shakes his head, offers a small, closed-mouth smile. "This is the first time I've heard that one. There was no meat pounder and no eggs. I hate eggs. That was just somebody's imagination working overtime."

I can't tell if it's the truth or not. He seems genuine, but maybe he's as good a liar as I am.

The corrections officer checks his watch again and says, "Time's up." Then he gives me the stop signal with his hand. "Stay where you are. Another officer will come and take you back to the waiting room."

As the officer is unlocking the handcuffs from the table, Lonnie Kraft looks over at me and says, "I left a present for you in the checkout room."

I can't imagine what it could be, but I say, "Thanks. That was real thoughtful of you."

"It's something I learned to do while I've been in here. It keeps me from going crazy."

As Lonnie Kraft is doing the little-baby-step walk to the door, he looks back at me and says, "I'm glad you came."

"Me, too," I say.

That's a lie, because now I feel pure awful. It would have been so much better if my father had been the way I'd always pictured him: big and mean and bad-mouthing Roxie and me and Harry, too. And that he really did kill his sweet mother with a meat pounder because she cooked his eggs wrong. This way I'll never know if he's rotting away in prison because his mother was just like me.

While I'm waiting for the other officer to come and get me, the voice in my head makes a surprise appearance and says, *Guess the apple doesn't fall far from the tree.*

My insides contract—bad. "Who are you?" I ask right out loud.

And he says what I've been afraid of since I killed Lester's father. *Haven't you guessed? I'm you. The real you.*

⫶ ⫶ ⫶

On the way home, Roxie doesn't ask me one single question about what was said in that room with the metal table. It's as though she's packed that part of her life away and intends to leave it there. The only thing she does say about our trip to Dannemora is "Do you feel better now?"

"Yeah, I do," I say so she won't think I wasted her time. The truth is, I don't know how to feel. I was kind of hoping I'd discover that some sinister relative was channeling thoughts through me and that an exorcism of some sort would smoke him out. Now I have to live with the fact that I'm as nuts as my grandmother, just regular old crazy.

I look over at Roxie and think how I've had her all wrong. She wasn't a tramp. I wonder why the guy in my head said that— pure meanness, probably. Then I remember what he just told me, and I realize that it was *me* being mean. The voice is me.

ꜟ ꜟ ꜟ

When I get home, I unwrap the package Lonnie Kraft left for me. It's a painting—the oil kind with the initials L.K. in the lower right-hand corner. It's beautiful: a field of daisies with a path going through the middle. I've always loved paintings with a path in them. You can imagine anything you want around the corner.

I start to hide it in the back of my closet. Then I change my mind and hang it over my desk, because in the deepest part of my heart, I believe him—that it was self-defense when he killed his mother.

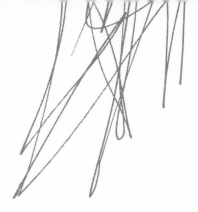

tick a lock.

It's the day before Thanksgiving, school's out, and Harry has made Belgian waffles for breakfast with the new waffle iron Roxie gave him for his seventieth birthday. Seventy seems so much older than sixty-nine, which he was just two days ago. When you read in the paper about the people who died and you see *70* after a person's name, you think, Oh, well, seventy— that's a good, long life. But it's not really, not for Harry, anyway. I can't even imagine living without him.

He puts my plate in front of me. The waffle is big and round and perfectly golden, with butter melting in each little pocket. He opens a container of maple syrup—real, not the fake kind— and starts pouring. "Say *when*," he instructs.

"When," I say as soon as syrup starts dripping off the side of the plate.

"You really like that stuff," he says. "There'll be plenty left for another waffle. I'll make you one."

"No, that's okay," I say. "I'll just eat what's left with a spoon."

Harry makes a *eeww* face. "My teeth hurt just thinking about it."

I take my first bite. "This is delicious, Harry," I say. "Where's Roxie?"

"She's sleeping in this morning. She stayed up late watching TV, and now she's taking it easy." I wonder how easy she could take it if she'd ended up with Lonnie Kraft or any man other than Harry. "I told her you and I will do the Thanksgiving grocery shopping. Is that okay with you?"

"Sure," I say, cheerful. I like to go grocery shopping with Harry. In fact, I like to do anything with him. If he asked me to go to the dump, I would say "I'd love to" and mean it.

⋮

As Harry and I are headed toward the entrance to the Price Chopper, I see Patty-Ann Thurston on her brand-new, bright-red tricycle, waiting for us. I haven't seen her since that day by the bridge, and a feeling of impending doom overtakes me when I think that she'll probably talk about what happened right in front of Harry.

"Hi, Maggie," Patty-Ann says. "How do you like my new bike? It has a basket and everything. My old one didn't." She points to the grocery bag in the basket. "I don't have to carry my stuff anymore."

"It's beautiful," I say. "I love the color."

I start to walk away, but Harry doesn't. He smiles at Patty-Ann and says, "That's a *great* bike."

"Sure is," Patty-Ann says. "I got it because of Maggie."

Harry looks at me, then back at Patty-Ann. "Really? How so?"

Well, this is *it*. I knew it would come eventually, but I didn't picture it happening at the Price Chopper. Mostly, I imagined the authorities showing up at our house and taking me away in handcuffs after they'd badgered Patty-Ann so long she finally told the truth.

"That's a secret between Maggie and me," Patty-Ann says. She makes a circular motion on her lips with her thumb and forefinger. "Tick a lock," she adds, grinning at me. Then she takes off on her bike without another word.

"What's this big secret you and Patty-Ann have?" Harry asks. He doesn't look suspicious, just curious.

"I have no idea," I lie. "If we have a secret, she's the only one who knows what it is."

"I haven't heard anybody say 'tick a lock' in years," Harry says, laughing.

"What's it mean?" I ask as we're entering the store.

"It's a slang expression—a promise that she'll never breathe a word to anybody."

Relief flows through me and, to make my lie more believable,

I add, "Not even to me, I guess." I turn and watch Patty-Ann disappear in the distance, thinking about the denim tote bag she is carrying—the one with the green trim and a huge safety pin holding the strap to the rest.

Harry smiles. "Well, Patty-Ann lives in her own world. It could be anything."

My heart is lighter than it's been since the bridge thing happened. I'd like to put this feeling in my pocket to save it, take it out when I need it. And all of a sudden, I'm starving. "Let's tackle that list, Harry, and make this the best Thanksgiving ever."

ⵏ ⵏ ⵏ

Harry and I are on our way home with the groceries. I don't know whether it's because I'm not worried about Patty-Ann blowing the whistle anymore or because I've been wondering about this since my visit to Lonnie Kraft and I just can't stand the suspense any longer, but I blurt out, "Harry? How did you and Roxie meet?"

The car slows and Harry's face drops, but he stays silent.

Now I'm sorry I mentioned it. I should have left things well enough alone. I've never seen him look so demolished. It's as though I just accused *him* of murdering Joe Matte.

He's tightened his grip on the steering wheel, and the muscles in his jaw are doing a little dance. "I was hoping you'd never ask," he says. He looks over at me with tortured eyes. "It's not something I'm proud of."

I've uncovered a crack in Harry's perfection, and it makes me feel sick to my stomach. Some things are supposed to be flawless and left alone, like those huge diamonds you see in museums— the ones they keep in glass cases with guards around.

I think how a few minutes ago Harry and I were happily picking out apples for the pie we're going to make and now he looks as though I've punched him in the gut. This is how fast a moment can fall down a rat hole.

"That's okay," I say, trying to sound as if I didn't hear his real answer and what he actually said was "We met on a Ferris wheel at a carnival, but I don't have time to tell you the whole wonderful story right now." Sometimes it's better to lie about a thing.

But Harry's not a liar like me. "No, it's *not* okay," he says, serious. "You deserve to know the truth."

I don't want to know the truth. I want things to stay the way they are.

"Your mother came to the funeral home to make arrangements for her parents after they were killed in the car accident."

"Oh." I look down at my jeans. The weatherman was wrong. It's too hot for jeans today. That's why I'm sweating.

The car's barely moving now. "She was all alone, just a kid a couple years older than you."

*Please, God. Don't let him tell me that he molested her. That he's really my father and they blamed Lonnie Kraft for what he did.* His face looks as if it's that bad, but if I don't let him say it, it won't be real. I have to get away from him. "Harry?"

"What is it?"

"Will you pull the car over? There's a Sunoco station coming up. I need to use their bathroom."

"Sure, but we're almost home."

"I can't wait."

We pull into the Sunoco lot and park near the back. As soon as the car stops, I reach for the door handle. "Mare, please let me finish," Harry says. "You're going to have to hear it sometime."

He's right. What difference will a few minutes make? It won't change anything. If I run home, he'll tell me when he gets there. I look over at his shirt, Clorox white. Roxie ironed it perfectly, sharp creases down the sleeves, light starch. He's wearing a tie, like he always does, one Roxie bought for his birthday: navy blue with a little burgundy design, fleur-de-lis, I think. I sit back, rest my fingers on the door handle, don't plan to say a word.

"Your mother didn't have any money," he continues. "Her parents didn't own much—not even their home—and her father wasn't the best at staying current with his bills, so he owed just about everybody in town."

What does this have to do with anything? "Didn't she have any relatives?" I ask.

"She had an aunt and uncle on her father's side. She'd never met them and didn't know where they lived. And I guess her father had pretty much used them up, anyway."

"So what happened? You haven't really told me *anything*."

My tone must have said "Get a move on" because he blurts out, "I made a deal with her."

"What kind of deal?" The sleazy kind between a dirty old man and a young girl you see on TV crime shows?

"I told her I'd pay her bills and provide proper burials for her parents if she'd . . ."

I look him up and down as though he's slime. "If she'd *what?*"

"Marry me."

"What?"

"She was nearly ready to have you, and desperate."

Time stands still as if someone pressed the pause button on my life. When the action starts again, my fingers move away from the door handle, and my insides calm down just a little. "So you blackmailed her?"

"That's not exactly blackmail, but it's . . . well . . . pretty close." He lowers his eyes. "As I said, I'm not proud of what I did."

"Why didn't you just bury her parents like you did Mr. Sullivan? They must have deserved it as much as he did."

"I would have, but she said she'd marry me as soon as I offered."

I know the answer to this, but I ask, anyway. "How old was she?"

"Eighteen."

"And how old were you?"

He hesitates as if he doesn't want to answer. "Fifty-four," he says as if he wishes the words would fall into a hole and disappear. Even though I've known their age difference forever and it's never bothered me, *those* two numbers sound really icky together.

"Why didn't you get married when you were younger?" I ask. "I mean, to somebody your own age."

Harry looks over at me, and color rises from his neck to his face. "I would have liked to."

"Well, then?"

He raises his eyebrows and shrugs. "I guess you could say I was the Lester Pint of my class."

No! That can't be. "But you told me how much you liked to dance and how you went to parties and everything."

"I did. All the girls liked to dance with me because I was good at it. Nobody could do the jitterbug as well. But when it came to the slow dances, the popular boys moved in and took my place."

I picture Harry tossing stones at a mean girl's window and her making fun of him. My voice softens. "What about college? Didn't you try to meet somebody there?"

"I was still the nerdy outcast, and nobody did the jitterbug anymore, so I pretended to be more interested in my studies than in dating."

"Oh." I can't think of anything to add.

"And after that I went to mortuary school to please my father. He wanted me to carry on the family business after he was gone. Can you think of a bigger turnoff than dating a funeral director?"

It wouldn't bother me because I'm used to it, but I guess most girls would find it pretty gross. "Probably not."

He sighs. "Anyway, the years went by and then your mother walked into my life."

I'm pretty sure I know the rest of the story, but maybe not. I look Harry straight in the eye. "You wanted a family, didn't you?"

He looks right back at me and tears up. "More than anything. I used to see couples with kids, and my heart would break because of what I didn't have. And when your mother came along, I got two children: one almost grown and a brand-new baby."

I start to ask him about the creepy part but stop. I can't get the words to come out.

"I didn't, Mare. Your mother and I . . . well . . . we've always been friends, but that's all."

I let out the breath I've been holding, and I can smell the apples in the backseat. They make me think of home and the good aroma of piecrust: golden brown and flaky. We'll peel and slice and add cinnamon and cloves and nutmeg and butter, and just thinking about it nearly makes me cry.

I nod to let him know I understand.

"I thought she'd find someone her own age and leave," he says, all matter-of-fact. "But she didn't. Maybe she never will."

"I think you're right," I say. As far as I can see, Roxie's perfectly happy right where she is.

Then Harry surprises me. "I believe your mother will always be crazy about Lonnie Kraft, but she loves you too much to do anything about it."

What?! No. Well, maybe. That could be why she didn't come in with me the day I went to the prison. It might have been too hard for her to see him. I don't say anything, just look at Harry and nod.

"Is it okay if we go home now?" Harry asks. "The guy who owns the station is giving me the evil eye. My tank's full, so I can't even buy gas."

"Yes," I say. "Let's go home."

❡ ❡ ❡

When I get to my room, I take Lonnie Kraft's painting down and put it in the back of my closet. I feel like a traitor to Harry having it on my wall. Then I go to the kitchen to help him put away the groceries and get started on the pie.

"You two were gone forever," Roxie says when she sees Harry and me emptying the bags onto the counter. "I hope you left enough time to make the pie and cranberry sauce. You can't do everything tomorrow."

I roll my eyes in my mind and try to make my smile look genuine. "Oh, we did," I say. "We have plenty of time."

I think how that desperate, pregnant eighteen-year-old girl is long gone. Then I wonder who got the better deal out of her visit to Feigenbaum's Funeral Home that day sixteen years ago. Roxie is pretty sly. Maybe she was then, too.

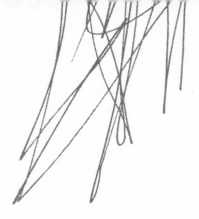

Thank you for everything.

Sometimes a thing surprises you so much that your eyes pop wide-open like a comic strip character. Roxie and I are Christmas shopping at the mall in Plattsburgh. We're at our last stop, Kay Jewelers, when I see Dr. Scott with a woman, a very pretty woman—my English teacher, Ms. Granger—and they're looking at engagement rings!

I grab Roxie's arm and drag her toward the door.

"Wait a sec!" Roxie says, trying to wrestle herself from my grip and still hold on to the shopping bags she's carrying. "We didn't get Harry's watch yet."

"Let's do that after lunch," I plead. "I'm starving, and this place is packed."

"Well, okay," Roxie agrees. "I'm hungry, too."

As soon as we're outside the store, I look through the window to see if Dr. Scott and Ms. Granger spotted us; but no, they're still engrossed in those rings. I would love to keep staring, though, because I haven't seen Dr. Scott in almost a month. Evidently, I've been doing a real good acting job, because he thinks I'm almost cured.

At the food court, Roxie chooses Taco Bell: grilled chicken burrito, caramel apple empanada, and coffee, black. I take a small Pepsi but don't touch a drop. When your imaginary future has just been shattered, your stomach rebels.

! ! !

When I get home, I decide to take Maud for a walk. Just seeing the leash makes her so happy that she nearly turns herself inside out. Today we go the opposite way from our regular route so she won't see Stanley. I am not in the mood for romance of any kind.

At first Maud tugs on the leash to tell me that I've made a mistake, but once we get going, she forgets Stanley and starts sniffing the ground. *Oh, boy,* she must be thinking. *I didn't know the world was this big with so many new smells.* Mostly when she is sniffing, there is nothing to see, just grass or sidewalk. And sometimes she rolls on the ground as if she's doing the backstroke so she can take the smell home with her to keep. I guess that for her, it's like putting money in the bank for a rainy day.

As I'm walking toward the Pints' house, I think of what

Harry told me about his growing-up years, and I feel bad about all the times I made fun of Lester in my head or outright ignored him. I wish I could find the girls who did that to Harry and give them a piece of my mind.

It's cold today. I can see my breath, and it reminds me of when Lester and I were little and we used to sit on his front step and pretend we were smoking cigarettes. We'd hold our imaginary Marlboros to our lips, inhale, then exhale and watch the white "smoke" rise into the freezing air. We were like newborn puppies. But then life got complicated: him with his brute of a father and me with whatever this thing is in my head.

I see Mrs. Pint walking down her sidewalk, on the way to the mailbox, probably. Too late to turn around—she's already seen me. Maud is full speed ahead, a new person to meet, another tail-wagging experience.

"Hi there, Mary," Mrs. Pint says. She bends down to scratch Maud behind her ears. "How have you been?"

"Fine," I say. Then I add, "Fine, thank you. And you?" because I know that's the proper way.

Mrs. Pint opens her mailbox, the expensive kind you see in fancy catalogs with scenes painted on the sides. Hers has pine trees that match the ones surrounding her house and the name Pint in fancy script, which makes that plain name look posh.

"I'm fine, too," she says. She takes a handful of letters that look like Christmas cards out of her mailbox.

"How's Lester?" I ask. I know he's okay, because I saw him yesterday in school. But what else is there to say?

"He's inside packing," she says, no vengeance in her voice because Lester and I are obviously not friends anymore. "We're moving to New York City right after Christmas."

I look around the yard. There's no For Sale sign, but maybe when you sell a house this beautiful, signs are tacky and you keep things private. "Oh, I didn't know that," I say, surprised.

"I've always wanted to live in Manhattan, and Lester will finish school there." When she looks over at the house, I do, too, and I see Lester watching us from an upstairs window. He doesn't even close the curtain fast like I would have done. But Mrs. Pint isn't looking at Lester. She's surveying the whole place. She sighs then says, "It's best to put Allenburg behind us and start fresh."

"Right," I agree. "That sounds like a good idea." Well, that was dumb. Why didn't I just say I'm sorry to hear that they're leaving?

Mrs. Pint pats me on the arm and says, "I realize that you and Lester have had a falling out, but I want to thank you for being such a good friend to him for so many years. He would have been a very lonely boy if it hadn't been for you."

I nod. "Oh, that's okay," I say. Lame. I wonder if I'll ever learn to talk like a regular person who has a brain.

Mrs. Pint starts walking toward her house but stops and says, "Mary?"

"Yes?"

At first she just stands there looking at me, but then she smiles a little. "Thank you for everything."

This time I don't think her thank-you has anything to do with Lester. I believe she's thanking me for her own self, for her fresh start, and it makes me feel creepy inside that she knows.

❗ ❗ ❗

When I get home, I lie on my bed and try to take a nap so this miserable day will go by faster. My body doesn't cooperate because I'm not tired. I stare at the crack in the corner of the ceiling that comes with the dry air of winter. It looks like one of those divining rods olden-day people used to find things underground, such as water and valuables and bodies.

Maybe if I read it'll make me sleepy. Just as I'm reaching for my book on the nightstand, my cell phone rings, so I grab that instead. Nobody ever calls me except Roxie. She probably wants me to come up to the attic or down to the basement to clean something.

"Hello?" I say, annoyed.

"Hi, Maggie." Abigail's tone is upbeat, as if she's trying to act as though the junk she's pulled lately never happened.

"Hi, Abigail." I hate that I'm glad it's her and that I'm sitting straight up, wondering what she wants.

"How have you been?" she asks.

"Who? Me?" Of course she means me. Who else would she be talking about? "Oh, fine. How about you?"

"Pretty good, I guess. I must say, though, that I've been better." She still sounds so much like her mother's daughter. I guess being part of the in-crowd didn't erase that.

"Oh, well, that's nice." This conversation sounds as if it's between two idiots.

"Actually, Maggie, I'm not good at all," Abigail says. "Jacob broke up with me, and I've been dropped from Allison Jamison's group."

Now we're getting somewhere. "That's too bad," I say, even though I feel like standing on my bed and doing a happy dance. "What happened with Jacob?"

"He told me he wanted to date other girls. And, Maggie, by *other girls* he meant Stephanie Price. He's actually been going out with her behind my back for weeks. When I pressed him about it, he finally told me the truth." Then she adds in a teacher's voice, "Stephanie had better set strict boundaries, is what I think."

Where have I heard that before? Even though Jacob's a total creep, a tiny thrill of revenge skitters up and down my backbone. "Well, that's just wrong," I say, trying to sound as supportive as possible.

"Of course I feel terrible," Abigail says with doom in her voice. "I thought he was *the one* and that we'd spend the rest of our lives together because . . . well, you know . . . because of what almost happened—what we almost had to do."

"Right," I say. He talked you into getting an abortion so he *wouldn't* have to spend the rest of his life with you. You just lucked out and didn't have to have one.

"He sure had my parents fooled," she says with bitterness in her voice. "He's such a charmer with grown-ups. Even my father liked him."

I think of how Maud acted the day Jacob came to my house. If she could take an IQ test, her score in the judging-people department would be in the genius category.

Abigail lowers her voice as though somebody might be eavesdropping. "Anyway, he's Stephanie's problem now. And you know the kind of reputation *she* has—it starts with a *w*, ends with an *e*, and rhymes with *more*." Poor Abigail, I think. Even though she has popular-girl looks, she's still the same dweeb who can't say words like *whore* out loud.

"Yeah," I lie. "She's a real slut." I don't even know who Stephanie Price is. All of Allison's cronies look the same to me. "So what happened with Allison?"

"Maggie, she is *so* shallow, you just wouldn't believe."

Yes, I would. "Shallow how?"

"It turns out the only reason those girls wanted me in their group was so that I could give them my mother's tests before they had to take them."

"Huh." I never would have guessed that.

"When I wouldn't, they got mad because they actually had to study. Then I told my mother what they were up to, and she gave them detention for a month."

For crying out loud. Abigail's hopeless. I try to sound sympathetic, though. "Well, what else could you do in a situation like that?"

"True," she says as though she thinks I'm being serious. "If they don't study, how are they going to learn anything?" She sighs. "Anyway, Maggie, it was a hard lesson to learn; but I've learned it, and I hope you can forgive me for . . . well . . . not spending as much time with you as I used to."

"I forgive you," I say, genuine.

She takes in a loud breath of air and lets it out slowly. "Oh, good," she says. "I thought maybe you'd hold a grudge."

I say nothing.

"Maggie?"

"Yeah?"

"Do you want to go get a Coke? We could walk to Stewart's—my treat."

"No thanks."

"Oh, so you're doing something?"

"I'm not doing anything."

"So later then?"

"No."

"But you said you forgave me."

"I did."

"Maggie, I don't understand."

This whole thing is making me tired. I think I'll be having that nap after all. "Look, Abigail," I say, straight-line serious. "I don't want to be friends anymore."

"How about if I come over to your house and we can talk about it?" There's desperation in her voice now.

"I just don't want to."

"But, Maggie!"

"I have to go now, Abigail. Please don't call me again."

I press the Off button on my phone and lie back down. Part

of me wishes that things could be the same between Abigail and me. But there's another part, the part that's thinking about her severe allergy to peanuts. If she chucked me again, it would be so easy to get revenge—for good.

This last thought scares me, and I tell myself that I'd never do anything to hurt Abigail.

## "The Thing Is".

I t's the last day before Christmas vacation, and I'm in English class. Ms. Granger is wearing the most beautiful diamond ring I've ever seen—emerald-cut—set in either white gold or platinum. Platinum, probably, because of how classy her fiancé is. I guess Dr. Scott couldn't wait until Christmas to give it to her.

Ms. Granger asked us to find a poem that described our lives, and today we're reading them to the class. When she had us write our own poems, they were so terrible, I guess she figured that if we read real ones, she wouldn't have to roll her eyes so much and go home with a headache.

I'm next, because everybody else has read theirs. They chose famous dead people such as Elizabeth Barrett Browning and Charlotte Brontë and Walt Whitman. And some picked funny poems by Ogden Nash and Dr. Seuss. But none of those poems told my story. So I searched the library until I found a poem by Ellen Bass, who I learned is not dead and lives with her family in California. The name of the poem is "The Thing Is." When I read it, I cried, because it was as if she had written it just for me. So instead of choosing a mindless ditty about a flawless girl with visions of springtime dancing in her head, I figured, What the heck. The other kids already think I'm a weirdo, and most of them won't listen, anyway. Besides, if Dr. Scott can't figure me out, I doubt if a bunch of high school students can.

I walk to the front of the class, take a second to compose myself, and then begin:

"The Thing Is"
to love life, to love it even
when you have no stomach for it
and everything you've held dear
crumbles like burnt paper in your hands,
your throat filled with the silt of it.
When grief sits with you, its tropical heat
thickening the air, heavy as water
more fit for gills than lungs;
when grief weights you like your own flesh
only more of it, an obesity of grief,
you think, *How can a body withstand this?*

Then you hold life like a face
between your palms, a plain face,
no charming smile, no violet eyes,
and you say, yes, I will take you
I will love you, again.

After I finish reading the poem, some of the kids snigger and Allison Jamison groans, and I hear one girl whisper "What's it mean?" to the boy next to her. But then the bell rings, and everybody scurries off to their next class.

As I head toward the door, Ms. Granger asks me to come to her desk. "That's such a lovely poem," she says. "And you read it beautifully. But, Maggie, is that what your life is really like?"

I imagine Lester and Abigail and Dr. Scott and the voice in my head and Lonnie Kraft and the people I've killed, and I think, *Yes, pretty much.* But I don't say it. I say, "No. My life is nothing like that. I just like dark stuff."

Ms. Granger smiles and says, "Well, I do enjoy the frightening stories you write. You have an amazing imagination!"

"I know," I say, smiling back at her. "My head is chock-full of gruesome ideas."

❢ ❢ ❢

"You've made some really good progress as far as coming to grips with your feelings about your mother," Dr. Scott says.

I smile at him, try to make it seem authentic. "I know," I say.

"Roxie's a really good person. And I think in my heart I knew all the time that she loves me and that she wouldn't leave."

Dr. Scott nods. "I agree. I knew once you opened up about what was bothering you, things would start to get better."

"I should have come clean sooner," I say. "I don't know why I waited. I guess I just didn't want to seem too selfish." I give him an embarrassed look. "Or too crazy."

"You're not crazy at all. You're a perfectly normal teenager."

Oh, if that were only true.

"And your mom said the nightmares have stopped completely. That's good!"

"Yup, they have." He doesn't need to know that I'm still sleeping in caskets—except now I make sure my iPhone is fully charged so I hear the alarm and get back upstairs before Roxie and Harry wake up.

I've been staring at Dr. Scott's beautiful new sweater throughout my whole session. It's a cream-colored Irish one that looks handmade—Ms. Granger, I bet. She seems like the kind of person who could do anything. Like if her brand-new husband called and said he was bringing a dozen people home for dinner in an hour, she would say, "Great, no problem. I'll whip up some crab cakes and a cheese soufflé." I want so much to hate her, but I can't. She's my favorite teacher ever. Sometimes you just have to let go of a dream.

"Looking forward to Christmas, Maggie?" Dr. Scott asks when our time is up.

"Yes," I say. "It's exciting."

"Think you'll get some pretty good loot?"

"Uh-huh. Harry's already given Roxie and me skis and season tickets to Whiteface. And there'll be some little surprises under the tree."

"Oh, wow. That's a real haul!"

I'd rather have the diamond ring. "Yeah, it's great. He's supergenerous."

"Does Harry ski?" Dr. Scott asks.

"Not anymore. He used to, but he broke his ankle the last time, so he doesn't go anymore."

Dr. Scott nods, looks as sad as I feel about Harry being left out. "Have you been skiing yet?" he asks.

"A couple of times on the bunny slope. We're going again on Saturday for another lesson on the real trails."

"I hope you have a great time."

"Thanks, we will."

"Well, have a nice Christmas, and I'll see you after the holidays."

"I'll see you next year," I say as I stand up.

Dr. Scott smiles. "Right—a brand-new year that should be fun and exciting for you."

Just as he's about to walk me to the door, his beeper goes off, so he waves bye to me instead. I spot a tiny wooden elephant on the table by the door. It's the exact same dark brown as Dr. Scott's eyes. I pick it up, rub it against my cheek, then put it in my pocket and close the door behind me. Now I'll have something of his to keep forever—not a diamond ring, but something. And I've heard that elephants whose trunks are facing up bring good luck.

I hope so. I sure could use some.

*I just hope that when I get there, they'll kill me.*

We have a ritual on Christmas Eve: order take-out pizza from Arnie's and decorate the tree. Ours is artificial, because Roxie claims the real needles ruin vacuum cleaners and she just bought a new one that was so expensive, one of the reviews on the Internet said that if it was a car, it would be a Bentley. If I ever have twelve hundred dollars, I am certainly not going to blow it on a vacuum cleaner! When I absolutely have to have one, I'll buy a Ford.

"Want the last piece of pizza, Harry?" I ask. "You've only had one."

"No, that's okay. You go ahead. I'm not really hungry." He's standing on a kitchen chair, putting the angel on top of the

196

tree. I've never asked him why he ignores the Jewish holidays but goes full steam ahead for the Christian ones. He must think it's important to Roxie and me. I'd be fine with Hanukkah and Passover and the other special days. I don't know about Roxie, though. She's never mentioned anything about her religious beliefs. Maybe she doesn't have any. I think, for her, Christmas and Easter are just excuses to get gifts.

Sometimes I wish I didn't believe in God. But I do. And I know he's up there watching every move I make. He's probably smacking himself on the forehead and thinking, *Where did I go wrong with that one?*

Roxie glances up at Harry and says, "Are you feeling all right? You look pale."

"I'm fine, just a little queasy is all." He adjusts the angel. "How's that?"

I step back. "Perfect," I say. "The whole thing is gorgeous."

Roxie stands next to me and agrees. "You're right. It's the prettiest one ever. Come see it, Harry. You did most of the work. Now it's time to relax and enjoy it. There's eggnog in the fridge."

"It *is* beautiful," Harry says when he's next to us. "And I hope you two don't mind, but I'm going to turn in. I think I have a touch of the stomach bug. I'll be fine tomorrow."

! ! !

Harry didn't have the stomach bug, and he was never fine again. The autopsy report stated that he suffered a massive heart attack around one o'clock on Christmas morning and *my* heart is so shattered, I can hardly breathe. It's as if I'm drowning in sorrow.

Unlike Mr. Sullivan, Harry was so well loved that the funeral home is overflowing with mourners. He can't be buried until the spring thaw, so he'll have to be put in a vault at the cemetery along with the others who died at an inconvenient time. When the service is over and nearly everybody has left the room, I stay by the casket and hold Harry's hand. I can't just leave him here alone. But then Roxie and Dr. Scott lead me out of the room and upstairs to my bed.

ɪ ɪ ɪ

It's a week after Harry's funeral, and Roxie and Dr. Scott are in the hospital hall, talking. I guess they don't think I can hear them because they're using regular voices. "She still hasn't said anything about trying to kill herself," Roxie says. "All she does is lie there. I've gotten her to eat a little soup but other than that, nothing. She can't go on like this much longer." Roxie starts to sob. "I should never have left those pills where she could get them. It's my fault."

"It's not your fault," Dr. Scott assures her. "If your pills hadn't been there, she would have tried another way. And she won't talk to me either." His voice is as worried as Roxie's. "She needs more help than we can give her."

"What do you mean?" Roxie asks. "Don't you think she'll get better eventually?"

"I do, but she's going to need intensive therapy and probably medication, at least for a while."

"Can't you do that?" Roxie asks.

"No. My specialty is anxiety, and I'm not licensed to prescribe medication. She'll need a psychiatrist for that."

"So what do I do?" Roxie's voice sounds frantic.

"I've spoken with Dr. Adams at the Brockman Psychiatric Hospital across the lake in Burlington. He said there's a bed available and that he'll treat her. He's the best psychiatrist I know of who specializes in depression."

"When will she leave?" Roxie asks. There's hopelessness in her voice.

"Today," Dr. Scott says. "She'll have to go by ambulance so they can monitor her."

Roxie must have nodded or given Dr. Scott some sort of yes signal, because he says, "I'll make the call."

Sadness has burrowed so deep inside of me that I don't care where I go. I just hope that when I get there, they'll kill me.

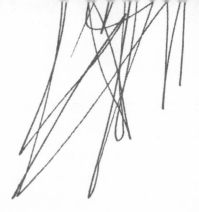

Love, Abigail.

"How are you feeling today, Maggie?" Dr. Adams says in his slow-talking way. He's old, even older than Harry was. His eyebrows are pure white, same as his hair, and they look like big, furry caterpillars. Sometimes when he stops to think and his face relaxes, I picture how he will look all done up in his coffin. Right now I can imagine his tired eyes being kept closed with eye caps and his mouth glued shut like Harry's assistant told me they do. And the embalming fluid will make him feel hard like a mannequin.

"I'm okay," I say. And I am. They're giving me pills to pep me up, and they're working—"Happy Pills" is what the kids here call them. I'm not exactly what you'd call happy; but I take my own shower now, and they don't have to force me to brush my teeth like they did when I first came two months ago.

Dr. Adams's office is the total opposite of Dr. Scott's. Everything is heavy and dark and real: leather, solid wood, expensive drapes at the windows. You can tell that he has made his fortune and is getting to the end of his working days, probably dreaming about moving to North Carolina or Florida like Harry used to do.

"Your mother called this morning," Dr. Adams says, cheerful. "She's looking forward to visiting you on Sunday."

"Oh, that's nice," I say, even though I don't care one way or the other. But it'll be the first time Roxie's been allowed to come since I got here, so I know I should appear to be happy.

"She's going to bring your dog."

Tears start when he mentions Maud. And the fact that I haven't thought about her until now makes me cry even harder. When I don't reach for it, Dr. Adams hands me the box of Kleenex that's on the corner of his desk.

"Maggie?" he says, kind. "Why does this make you so upset?"

"Because I love Maud," I sob.

"There has to be more to it than that. Will you tell me what it is?"

"Harry gave her to me."

Dr. Adams nods. He doesn't take notes like Dr. Scott, just listens.

My sobs have stopped, and now I'm doing that gasping,

hiccupping thing. "On my tenth birthday," I add. "He brought her home in a wicker basket with a pink bow tied to the handle." I laugh a little, which feels wrong. "Harry said it looked like he was giving me a basket full of ears and feet."

Dr. Adams chuckles. "What kind of dog is she?"

"A basset hound."

"Ah," he says. "Harry was right. When basset hounds are little, they do look like they're all ears and feet."

"She used to trip over her ears and fall down," I say, and now I'm crying again.

"What did your mother think about Maud?"

I wipe my eyes then blow my nose. "She didn't like her."

"Why not?"

"She thought dogs were dirty."

"You just said 'thought.' Did she change her mind?"

I nod. "Yeah. Now she loves her almost as much as I do."

"What changed?" Dr. Adams keeps his voice in a monotone. Maybe shrinks are taught to do that in college because Dr. Scott did, too, only not quite as much.

"Maud crawled into Roxie's heart just like she did mine."

Dr. Adams leans back in his chair. "How do you feel about Roxie's heart?"

"I think she keeps a shield around it."

"Why do you suppose she does that?"

I know the answer because Dr. Scott and I talked about it. "She has a hard time letting people get too close."

"What people?"

"Me."

"Why do you think that is?"

"I don't know. Is it okay if we stop for today?"

! ! !

When I get back to my room, I find a letter on my pillow. I know it's from Abigail even before I look at the return address because of the turquoise ink she always uses when she writes social things. She calls it her trademark, as if she's a superstar who gives out autographs.

*Dear Maggie,*

*I'm writing to say how sorry I am about your stepfather.*
*When I read the news in the paper, I noticed that he was*
*70 years old! He certainly had a good long life.*

*Now I'm going to try to cheer you up by telling you*
*what is happening here in Allenburg. First on the list is that*
*I have a new boyfriend. His name is Jonathan Miner, and*
*he is a senior who has his own car and can drive at night.*
*He is so much more mature than the boys in our class. He*
*treats me like a lady and lets me make all the decisions*
*about how far we go and how fast. I want you to know that*
*I am being VERY careful in that department. I am now*
*on the pill (my mother doesn't know, of course!), so there's*
*no chance of you-know-what happening. Tonight, Jonathan*
*is taking me to Plattsburgh to a play at the college and then*
*afterward we are going to a party at a fraternity house where*

*one of Jonathan's friends lives. My mother does NOT know about the party part. I haven't decided what to say when I get home so late, but I will think of something. She'll be right there by the door wanting to know every little thing that happened. You're lucky in that respect. Your mother has always left you pretty much alone. That must be nice!*

*Well, you are NOT going to believe this!!!! Allison Jamison got expelled from school for cheating on the SATs! My mother was one of the monitors, and she saw Allison take out her iPhone to look up an answer. Of course, iPhones are not allowed, but I guess Allison doesn't think the rules apply to her. Anyway, my mother told my father, and he threw her out of school for a whole week. After that, I don't know what will happen as far as Allison taking the SATs again. She plans to go to Vassar, but we'll see about that. When I remember how she treated me, I think of the old saying "What goes around comes around." Some people just deserve the bad things that happen to them. Don't you think so???*

*Now for JACOB!!! He was going out with Carrie-Ann Sanders and now she's gone. Word around school is that she has transferred to Deerfield Academy. IN THE MIDDLE OF THE SCHOOL YEAR??? I think you and I both know that she's more likely in a home for pregnant teens.*

*Oh, I forgot to tell you something when I was writing about me. I had my hair cut!! I can tell you this much. I*

*thought long and hard before I decided to take that plunge.*
*If they get Seventeen magazine where you are, look on page*
*86. The girl on the right (the pretty blond one) has the same*
*style, only mine's not quite that short. You will see it in*
*person when you get home.*

    *Well, I'd better close now because I have to finish getting*
*ready for my date with Jonathan. I am done with my shower*
*and hair and makeup. Now I just have to get dressed and*
*voilà! All set to go.*

    *I hope that your stay in that place will clear the air*
*between you and me and that things will go back to the way*
*they used to be.*

    *If they let you write letters, I'd be thrilled to hear from you.*
*Love,*
*Abigail*


This girl is totally clueless! I sigh, shake my head, tear her
letter into tiny pieces, and drop them into the wastebasket.

Like water in a mud pie.

I t's 11:30 on Sunday morning, and I'm sitting on my bed reading *Bastard Out of Carolina* when Roxie appears at my door with Maud. At first they both stand there like maybe they're in the wrong place, but then Maud sees me and comes running. I get off my bed, scoop her up, and hug her so tight she makes a little wheezing sound. Then Roxie comes over and wraps her arms around us both. This feels weird, because Roxie's never been very touchy-feely. I don't know how to react, but Maud does. She slobbers both our faces until the group hug ends.

"I'm glad the sixty days are over so now I can visit," Roxie says. She lowers her voice. "That seems like a silly rule. You'd think they'd want parents to come as often as possible." She sighs. "Well, they must have their reasons."

"I suppose so," I say with no enthusiasm, and I feel a little guilty that I haven't missed my mother at all. But I guess it's hard to miss something you never really had. Dr. Adams has helped me understand that since Roxie was so young when she had me and that her husband was more like her father, it makes sense in her mind to think of me as a sister rather than a daughter. My feelings have been shimmying around that one, but I'm pretty sure I'll come to terms with it eventually.

"You have your own room!" Roxie says, overly excited as she does a complete three-sixty on the stiletto heel of her knee-high leather boot—black to match her purse. Those boots are brand-new, just like her coat and purse and gloves even. "It's pretty," she adds. "I like that the drapes match the bedspread."

"Looks like you've been shopping," I say with a bite to my voice.

She glances down at her outfit, and at first I think she's going to lie and say, "Oh, this old thing? I've had it for years." But she doesn't. Instead, she says, "Yes, do you like it?"

No, I don't like it. It's gaudy and ugly; and even if that is a Coach purse, it had to be the cheapest-looking one in the store: all shiny brass buckles and fringe like on a cowboy jacket. And that coat: bright red and black squares. It reminds me of a check-erboard. "It's nice," I say. It took a lot of effort to make those two words sound halfway sincere. Doesn't she know that you don't go shopping for hooker clothes when your husband has just died?

Roxie sits on my bed and pats a spot next to her. "Come tell me what you've been doing. It's so good to see you up and dressed." She holds out my book, looks at the title, and frowns. "Where did this come from?" she says with disgust in her voice.

"I got it from the library."

"They have a library here?"

"Yes. A nice one."

"This doesn't look like something a young girl should be reading."

I take the book and slide it under my pillow. "It's fine, Roxie. It's on our reading list at school." That's a lie, but she won't check. I doubt that she'll even remember. I've never seen Roxie read a book in my whole life. But then I think of the part in Dorothy Allison's book where Bone's mother chooses her slimeball husband over her, and I rein in my anger because Roxie chose me.

"Okay then. So tell me some news," she says, trying to sound excited.

I'm in a mental institution. How much news could there be? "Dr. Adams is already weaning me off my antidepressants" is all I can think of.

"Great! That must mean you'll be coming home soon."

"He says it'll be a few more weeks. He wants to make sure I don't go back to where I was once I'm off the meds."

Roxie gives me a questioning look.

"Pills."

"Oh, right," she says. "I knew that. I just forgot. How about if I take you out for lunch?"

Well, I didn't expect this, and at first it feels as if she's trying to rip off the blanket I've been wrapped in since I got here. "I don't think I can."

"I asked at the front desk, and the woman said it's fine."

I'm not sure I'm ready for real people yet. "I don't know. Maybe we could just eat in the dining room here. The food's really good." And it is. Their lasagna is the best I've ever tasted.

"It would do you good to have a change of scenery," Roxie adds. Maybe she's the one who wants the change of scenery, because now she has her eyes glued to the bars on the windows.

"But we can't take Maud into a restaurant." That'll do it. Roxie hates fast food, so she'll want to go to a sit-down place. She can sit down here.

"Then we'll go to a drive-through and eat in the car."

I can see I'm not going to win this one. "Okay, I guess. I'll get my coat."

꜏ ꜏ ꜏

Roxie was right. It does feel good to have a change of scenery. It's one of those perfect winter days when the sun is so bright it sprinkles the snow with diamonds. And I didn't realize until now how pretty the building is. I certainly was in no shape to admire the architecture the day they brought me here.

Now we're heading down a long driveway with tall trees

bordering both sides—maple, I think, but it's hard to tell when they don't have their leaves on.

"We'll just drive till we find a place," Roxie says. "Is that okay with you?"

"Sure."

I look over at her made-up face and wonder how she can be back to normal so soon. At first I want to ask her if she ever really cared for Harry. But I think I already know the answer, because I asked Dr. Adams about it. She was too old to love him like a father and too young to love him like a wife. I guess he was just a friend—her only friend.

I think the guilt about the people I killed is mixed in with my grief for Harry, like water in a mud pie. That's probably why it's taking me so long to get better.

"Have you gone to see Lonnie Kraft yet?" I ask without looking at her.

Her back straightens, and she stares straight ahead at the road—a country one with no houses in sight. "I have," she says, plain.

"I thought so."

Silence from her.

At first it makes me angry, but then I remember that Harry knew how she felt about Lonnie Kraft all along. If it didn't bother him, why should it bother me? "I'm glad," I say.

She looks over—to see if I'm serious, I think—still says nothing, though.

"Roxie?"

"What?"

"I don't think Lonnie Kraft killed his mother on purpose. I think, like he told the jury, he was just defending himself when she came at him with a knife."

The quiet in the car booms like a bass drum.

"And, Roxie?"

"Yes?"

"You know the painting he gave me the day I visited him in prison?"

She nods.

"It's in the back of my closet. I want you to have it. It would mean more to you than it does to me."

Mascara tears stream down her face, and she doesn't do anything to wipe them away. "Thank you," she says. And the emotion in those words proves that Harry was right. She *has* been crazy about Lonnie Kraft all these years.

Well, there's no doubt about it —
I'm going straight to hell.

I t's been a week since Roxie's visit, and when I return from my session with Dr. Adams, I see a letter on my pillow and think it's from her. But, no, as I get closer, I see the turquoise ink.

> *Dear Maggie,*
>
> *I had hoped that you would reply to my last letter since that's what you are supposed to do when someone makes the effort to send you one. It's not like an e-mail where you can just press Delete and pretend that you didn't receive it.*
>
> *In any case, I will make this letter as interesting as possible to help you pass the time.*

*Remember when I told you about my date with*
*Jonathan—the play and the frat party? Well, that*
*night turned into a disaster. Number one—the play was*
*horrible. It wasn't even an official one that a real writer*
*did. It was by a college student who had better think twice*
*about his choice of occupations. If he thinks he will be able*
*to support himself by writing bad plays, he is in for a sad*
*awakening.*

*Now for the party: All it consisted of was BEER,*
*DRUGS, and SEX!!! Maggie, you probably won't believe*
*this, but people were having sex all over the place. There*
*was bare skin on display EVERYWHERE! And by*
*skin, I mean the kind that is supposed to stay covered in a*
*public place. Plus, I hate to even tell you this, but Jonathan*
*is not the person I thought he was. When he found out that I*
*wasn't going to join in the "fun," he left me sitting alone and*
*hooked up with a college girl—and I think you can imagine*
*what I mean by "hooked up." But I was not about to make*
*our sex life a public display of affection or PDA as it's*
*commonly called!!!*

*Things got so bad that I finally gave in and phoned my*
*mother to come get me. When I was safely out of there, she*
*put in an anonymous call to the police department to report*
*what was going on. I feel bad that Jonathan got arrested, but*
*my mother thinks it will be a blessing in disguise since it will*
*nip his self-destructive behavior in the bud. Now that he's*
*back in school, he's not talking to me, and he has convinced*

*most of the students to ignore me, too, which I think is juve-*
*nile, especially since he is a senior. This is all right with me*
*because now I have plenty of time to volunteer at the hospital*
*in Plattsburgh, and that will look good on my application to*
*medical school.*

*That's right, Maggie!! I've decided to become a doctor*
*instead of a math professor—a cosmetic dermatologist to be*
*more precise. Did you even know there was such a thing?*
*I didn't either until I read an ad for one in the newspaper.*
*What they do is specialize in keeping their patients looking*
*young. Doesn't that sound like a great way to help people? I*
*think so, too!*

*This next part is going to make you wonder what the*
*world is coming to. Allison Jamison is being allowed to*
*retake the SATs in May! Can you believe it? As it turns*
*out, her father has friends on the school board. It just shows*
*that you can commit a crime and get away with it!!! I, for*
*one, don't think that's right, and I'm sure you don't either.*

*Here's something exciting! A new activity for me is*
*cooking. I have a whole shelf of cookbooks, and I watch the*
*Cooking Channel as often as I can. Tonight I'm going to*
*serve baby back spareribs with an orange-molasses glaze*
*(homemade, not from a jar), basmati rice (I'll explain*
*what that is when you get home), and cauliflower topped*
*with a Gruyère cheese sauce. And for dessert? A cinnamon*
*streusel Bundt cake—baked in a castle-shaped pan from*

*Williams-Sonoma—my new favorite catalog. I will teach*
*you everything I know when you get home. I realize you've*
*already learned a lot about cooking. But this is the*
*GOURMET style!*

*So, Maggie, I can't think of anything else to say that*
*would be as interesting as what I have already written.*

*I'd love to hear about your activities!!*

*Love,*

*Abigail*

I don't even bother to tear up the letter this time, just drop
it into the wastebasket and think how Abigail is so turning into
her mother. And that's a pretty sad fate.

ꞮꞮꞮ

Just as I'm thinking of heading downstairs to watch TV, the girl
who has the room next to mine comes in. Her name is Maizie Gardner. She's been in this hospital for months but just got
moved to this wing a few days ago. We're already pretty good
friends. It's funny how that happens. You can know some people
for years and never connect; and then once in a while a person
walks into your life, and it seems as though you've known them
forever. Maizie lives in Plattsburgh with a foster family, but her
birth parents live about ten miles from Allenburg. And from the
little Maizie's told me, they're total losers.

"Hey, Mags," Maizie says as she plops on my bed next to me.

"What's goin' on?" She's tiny and built like a boy, so the mattress hardly moves.

I look at her and roll my eyes. *Her* eyes are the same dark brown as her hair and her skin.

"That exciting, huh?"

"How about you?" I ask.

"Well, there's no doubt about it—I'm going straight to hell. I might as well call ahead and make a reservation."

I giggle. "What'd you do this time?"

"I swore at the nurse."

"Which one?"

"Stewart."

This surprises me, because Abby Stewart is one of the nicest people here. "How come?" I ask. I haven't known Maizie long enough to figure out why she's so mad at everybody.

"Ah, she was on my back about making my bed wrong and not showing up for meds on time." She raises her eyebrows. "You ever get in trouble with her?"

I shake my head. "No," I say, "not really." I've never been in trouble with her at all, so the "not really" part was just for show.

Maizie play-punches me in the arm. She's an exercise nut, so it hurts a little. "You're such a goody-goody."

"Yeah, I know," I say. "I'm pathetic."

"I swear that Stewart woman's soul is as cold as the bodies in a graveyard."

My heart stops.

She puts her hand on my arm. She's wearing a silver thumb

ring—no other jewelry. "Oh, God. I'm sorry. I forgot about your father."

"That's okay," I say. And it is. I know she didn't mean it, and I wonder how long Harry's death is going to make me feel as though a big part of me is missing.

She shakes her head. "I should just wear duct tape over my mouth."

"But you wouldn't be nearly as much fun," I say.

She *is* fun, and I'm not exactly sure why her bad-girl personality draws me to her, but it does. Then I think a little more. Why wouldn't it? Compared to me, Maizie Gardner is a saint.

There's silence for a minute but then I decide to ask Maizie something I've been curious about since she moved into the room next to mine. "Umm...I was just wondering. . . ."

"About what?"

"You don't have to answer if you don't want to."

"I know that. What is it?"

"How come you got moved from your old wing?"

She laughs. "I was afraid you were going to ask me something hard."

"Well, I thought you might not want to tell me."

"They moved me because I got better. Not all better, but a lot better than I was."

"Oh. That's good." What more is there to say?

"Maggie, when I came here I was totally crazy. My foster parents found a letter I'd written about how I thought I'd been chosen to take all the evil people from Earth to another planet."

She stares at her hands then goes on. "When I got here, they put me on the acute floor—that's where they keep the sickest patients; some of them never leave that wing."

"But *you* did."

"I was lucky. The medicine's working."

"So you'll be going home soon?"

Maizie's happy expression changes to dismal. "Yeah," she says with gloom in her voice. "I'm not sure when, but it won't be too long."

I think how anxious I am to get out of here and wonder what awful thing is waiting for Maizie when *she* leaves.

! ! !

It's my last night here, and I'm in bed thinking about going home and how weird it'll be without Harry there. Then I picture him in heaven all well and happy. He and God are sitting in La-Z-Boys in the sunniest spot up there, and they're shooting the breeze as if they're best pals. Like God, Harry has a bird's-eye view of everything that goes on down here. Right now, he's pointing at me and bragging about how great I am.

God glares straight at me and shakes his head a little, but he doesn't say anything to Harry. Maybe talking bad about people isn't allowed up there. I appreciate this, but I'm still angry at God for what he did. When he reached down and took Harry, he yanked my heart out by the roots and stomped it flat with his big, old, holy foot. I'm not afraid of him anymore, though, because he's already done the worst possible thing he could do to me.

I *do* hope that Harry gets cozy enough with God so that he can convince him to transfer some points from Harry's plus column to mine for future use so we can be reunited someday.

I sure am going to need them.

*I know what I have to do.*

"How does it feel to be going home today?" Dr. Adams asks. We're sitting in his office, and he's dressed casually because it's Saturday. I think it's so sweet of him to come in special to give me a send-off.

"Good," I say, true. "I can't wait to see Maud."

Dr. Adams runs his tongue over his top lip and hesitates a bit. "What about Roxie? Will you be happy to see her?"

"Oh, *sure*. Of course."

"Do you think you two will have a better relationship now?"

"I do." I'm not just saying that either. "It'll be fun to have a sister to hang around with. I've always wanted one."

Dr. Adams gives me a knowing smile. I return it.

"Well, I'll tell you this much," he says, "everybody here is going to miss you. The staff thinks you're the kindest, most cooperative patient they've ever worked with."

I'm feeling great, really flying high; but then there's a buzzing in my head, and suddenly I hear that old, familiar voice: *Now ain't that sweet? If he knew the truth about you, he'd croak, right here and now.*

I struggle to keep my face regular, hope that Dr. Adams didn't notice the startled expression on my face. The guy in my head has left me alone the whole time I've been here. But now that I'm going to reenter my life, I guess he is, too. "Thanks, Dr. Adams," I say. "Everybody here's been terrific."

"I'm glad, Maggie. I have a feeling that you're going to do just fine. I'll hand you back to Dr. Scott, and you two can pick up where you left off."

"That's good news," I say in a professional tone because Dr. Adams is the formal type. The thought of seeing Dr. Scott again makes me forget the voice for a moment. I put my hand in my pocket and touch the little wooden elephant I took from Dr. Scott's office. I carry it around with me all the time.

"It's been a real pleasure, Maggie," Dr. Adams says. And that's it. He gets up from his chair, shakes my hand, and sends me on my way.

❢ ❢ ❢

Maizie's waiting on my bed when I get back from Dr. Adams's office. "So, how was your meeting?" she asks. "Did old Roger give you the heave-ho?"

"Yup," I say. "I'm a free woman."

"Lord," she says. "That man has to be a hundred. I'm always afraid he'll keel over in the middle of a sentence."

"I like him," I say.

She looks at me, surprised. "You do? Why?"

I shrug. "Because he's nice."

"Oh, really?" There's anger in her voice. "How do you know what he's like when he's home alone with his wife? Or when he was younger, how do you know that he didn't beat the crap out of his kids? Or that he's cleaned up his act just so he can get his only daughter back? Nice on the outside doesn't always mean snot."

*Whoa, Maggie,* the voice in my head says. *This poor kid's led a rough life. She needs help. Your help. Get my gist?*

Yes, I do get his gist, but I try to keep my thoughts on Maizie. Why did she wait until I was leaving to tell me what's bugging her so badly? I know she's describing her own father, and the thought of what she must have gone through makes me feel sick. I scoot back on the bed, lean against the wall. "What did he do to you?" I ask in a low voice.

She looks at me with tears in her eyes—more bitter than sad. "You know all the stuff they warn us about in health class and the junk you hear about on those news shows where the kids have endured years of abuse?"

"Yes."

"Well, you can check off every one of those boxes for my father."

*A man like that doesn't deserve to live.* This time the voice gives me a sharp jab in the head.

"And my mother's no better," Maizie continues.

"She abused you, too?"

"No, but she pretends it's not happening so he won't turn on her. Always has."

*Oh, brother. Maggie, you really have to rescue this girl.*

"I know," I whisper. "I know."

"How about your foster family?" I ask Maizie. "What are they like?"

"They're great."

"So why don't you stay with them?"

She stares at me as though she can't believe what I just said. "You don't know how the system works, do you?"

I shake my head. "No."

"My father went to anger management classes, and he's playing the good-guy act to the hilt. The court believes he's turned his life around and deserves another chance. When the judge sends you back to your birth parents, you have to go."

"Well, maybe those classes did cure him," I say.

Maizie looks at me as if I should be going to *idiot* classes. "When he came to visit a week ago, he twisted my arm so far back I thought it was going to break. Then he got in my face and told me to quit acting nuts."

"Why didn't you tell one of the nurses? Or Dr. Adams?"

"He didn't leave a mark this time. Besides, he said if I blabbed again, he'd kill me." There's terror in her eyes now. "He means it, Maggie. I know he means it."

*You gotta get rid of him. You gotta get rid of him real soon.*

"You're right," I answer in my head.

There has to be something else Maizie can do. "You're old enough to run away," I say as if I've just solved her problem.

"Run where?"

My shoulders drop. "I don't know. I just thought . . ."

"Mags, there's no way out for me." Tears have started again, this time a stream of them. "Last night I dreamed that their house burned down. This morning I wished it was true. They don't have insurance, so they'd have to go live with my grandmother. If they didn't have anyplace to live, I know she'd take them in. She hates kids, though, and she never liked me, so I bet I could return to my foster family. They said I'll always be welcome there."

Just as I'm thinking about what Maizie said, Roxie sashays into the room wearing a smile, a pair of leggings, and a brown leather jacket—fake, I'm sure, because, despite everything else, she's definitely an animal advocate, which I really like. "Hi there, Mary-Magdalene. Ready to come home?"

I look at Roxie's happy face and back at Maizie's hopeless one and have no idea what to do. Then, to top it off, the guy in my head decides to add to the confusion with *Get her birth parents' address! Now!*

But before I can think, Maizie wipes her tears with her sleeve and is already off the bed and halfway across the room. "Roxie," I say, "this is my friend Maizie."

Just as Roxie starts to respond, Maizie's gone; and all I can think of is the pain in her eyes when she turned and glanced at me on her way out the door.

Roxie looks at me, confused. "She a pretty little thing, but she must be terribly shy."

"She is," I lie. "That's why she's here. She has a social phobia." When you are in a place like this, you pick up the lingo fast.

"I see," Roxie says as if she knows what that is.

"Where's Maud?" I ask, disappointed.

"I left her at the groomer's. She's going to have a bath and her nails clipped. She wants to look her best when you get home."

I laugh because it's cute of Roxie and because when I really think about it—about going home to my sweet little Maud who loves me no matter what—I am so happy to be leaving this place.

"I thought we could drive over to Lake Placid, have lunch, then do a little shopping," Roxie says. "They have a J.Crew and a Banana Republic. You'd look great in their clothes. They're real classy, like you."

"Sounds like fun," I say without much enthusiasm. I bet Maizie's never had anything classy to wear in her whole life. And now all she has to go home to is misery.

! ! !

225

"Well, there it is," Roxie says, pointing to a brand-new black VW Beetle with a tan convertible top. "I'm so glad you finally decided to drive again." She hugs me, genuine. "And happy belated birthday!"

"Thanks," I say. "I love it!"

She hands me the keys and starts walking toward the passenger side of the car. "Let's get out of here," she says, upbeat.

"Yes, let's," I reply. As I start toward the driver's side, there's another jab, much stronger this time, making my head feel as if it's about to split wide-open. I glance at the building—at Maizie's empty window. My mood sinks when I think how she's going to have to live with her creep of a father.

Just then the sun goes behind the only cloud in the sky long enough to get my attention. When I look up, it comes out again, and I truly believe that Harry's telling me he's watching. I even feel a warm touch on my cheek. It might only be the sun, but it's as if Harry's hand is comforting me. As if he knows what I'm going through. As if he knows I can't walk away from Maizie. I know what I have to do.

"Roxie," I say. "I'll be right back. I forgot something."

*Now you're cooking.*

"Okay," Roxie says, "but hurry. I'm starving."

When I get to Maizie's room, she's lying on her bed, staring at the ceiling. "Miss me already?" she says when she sees me.

I laugh a little, sit on the chair next to her. "My mother's signing me out, so I thought I'd wait in here."

"Good."

*Ask her about her parents. You need to know when you can make your move.*

"Great idea," I say in my head. "You always know exactly what to do."

*Glad you're beginning to realize that.*

I look around the room as if I'm trying to think of what to say.

"You seem nervous," Maizie says. She sits up and leans against her headboard. "Something bothering you?"

"Nah. I'm just a little worried about how my mom and I are going to get along now that my stepfather won't be there."

*C'mon, Maggie. Get to it! Enough of this chitchat.*

"But you're so lucky," Maizie says. "Your mother seems to like you." She looks down at her hands. "And there's nobody there to smack you around."

Well, now I feel pure terrible. Here I am complaining about nothing, and Maizie's problems are so big. "You're right," I say. It's just that my mother's always home, and I can picture her hovering over me, making sure I don't go off the rails again." I look at Maizie, try to sound nonchalant when I say, "How about your parents? Are they home all the time?"

*That's more like it.*

Maizie shakes her head. "No, nobody's home during the day. My father works at the gas station, and my mother's hooked on the casino in Akwesasne, so she doesn't get home till late." She looks straight into my eyes. "It's nights mostly that I worry about."

*Bingo! Now we know when you can do it. We just have to figure out how. Maybe poison this time. There's a jug of weed killer in your garage. You could break into their house and douse her parents' food with it.*

"That might work," I reply under my breath, even though it's a stupid idea. That stuff smells so horrible; nobody would eat it.

"My mother left my dog home today," I say in a sad voice.

Maizie shrugs. "But you'll see her soon."

"Yeah, that's true. How about your parents? Do they have any pets?"

*What's this got to do with anything?* the voice says, disgusted. *We both know you're not going to kill any pets.*

"I know," I say under my breath. "I just don't want this to sound like the third degree."

*Well, okay then. But get a move on!*

"No, no pets," Maizie replies. "I always wanted a cat, but my mother's allergic."

"You know, I just thought of something," I say, fake cheery. "You told me your parents' house isn't that far from mine. I can come over and see you when you get home if you give me their address."

"There's no real address—just Stony Lonesome Road. Theirs is the old, dilapidated house at the very end."

I glance at my watch. "Well, I'd better go. My mother's probably ready by now."

*You know what you have to do,* the voice says, bossy. *Go do it!*

I look at Maizie. "I was just wondering. Is their house brick or wood or what?"

*Good grief, Maggie! Who are you? Perry Mason?*

"It's wood," Maizie says.

I think how fast an old wooden house would burn down.

*What difference does it make what the house is made of? The weed killer will do the job even if they live in a tent. And listen to me, girl,* he adds, his voice edgy, impatient. *I'm helping you out here.*

I hear the voice's words, but I ignore them. I think instead of everybody who really *has* tried to help me. Dr. Scott. Dr. Adams. Lonnie Kraft. Patty-Ann. Even Roxie. Abigail, too, in her own lopsided way. And Harry—especially Harry. Knowing I have all these people in my corner makes me feel strong. Stronger than the pain in my head, even though it's throbbing like crazy now.

"I'm not going to use weed killer," I whisper with as much gall as I can muster. "That's the dumbest idea I've ever heard."

*What are you talking about?* the voice says, astonished. *It's a perfectly good idea.*

"No, it's not. It's stupid."

*But . . . but . . . you know what you have to do, right?* The voice is almost gasping—as if it's running out of air.

Maizie's looking at me as if I might not be well enough to go home after all. "Why do you want to know what the house is made of?"

I head toward the door. "No reason," I say. "No reason at all."

On my way back to the car, I think that after killing three men, burning down an empty house to save a friend seems pretty tame. I just hope that when I do it, Harry and God will be off bowling or playing cards. But even if Harry does see me, I'm sure he'll understand.

But what about the voice? I don't know what it is or where it came from. I do know for sure it's not me. It can't be me. I don't want to do those bad things. It doesn't even sound like me. And who's that Perry Mason guy? Never heard of him!

*You know what you have to do,* the voice says again; but this time in an even quieter tone, so soft I can barely hear him. And it surprises me, but my head is totally clear—no pain at all.

"Yes, I do know what I have to do," I say right out loud, imagining Maizie happily back with her foster family and her parents staring at their smoldering shell of a home.

I touch the elephant in my pocket. "I do know what I have to do. And with a little luck, I'm going to do it."

# Acknowledgments

A special thank-you to my agent, Wendy Schmalz. She's savvy and funny and a pleasure to work with.

My deepest gratitude to my editor, Melanie Kroupa. Sometimes you wonder what you did to have something really great happen in your life. That's how I felt when Melanie said yes to my story.

Many thanks to everyone at Amazon Children's Publishing who worked so hard to create this book.

Ellen Bass allowed me to include her lovely poem "The Thing Is" from her book *Mules of Love* (BOA Editions, 2002). Thanks, Ellen. It's still my favorite.

A big thank-you to Dr. Paul Foxman, Sharon McBride, and Patricia Peters. Your help and expertise were invaluable.

To Bob, Rob, and Sarah. Thank you for being my family. I love you.